ANTIQUES FIRE SALE

A TRASH 'N' TREASURES MYSTERY

ANTIQUES FIRE SALE

BARBARA ALLAN

THORNDIKE PRESS

A part of Gale, a Cengage Company

LIBRARY OF CONGRESS CIP DATA ON FILE.
CATALOGUING IN PUBLICATION FOR THIS BOOK
IS AVAILABLE FROM THE LIBRARY OF CONGRESS

ISBN-13: 978-1-4328-8286-0 (hardcover alk. paper)

Published in 2020 by arrangement with Kensington Books, an imprint of Kensington Publishing Corp.

Printed in Mexico
Print Number: 01   Print Year: 2020

To our readers
past, present, and future

Brandy's quote:
Liar, liar, pants on fire
nose as long as a telephone wire

— playground song

Mother's quote:
O for a Muse of fire that would ascend
the brightest heaven of invention

— William Shakespeare, Henry V

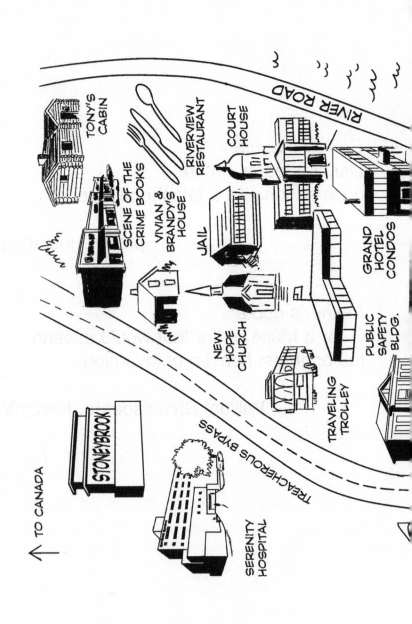

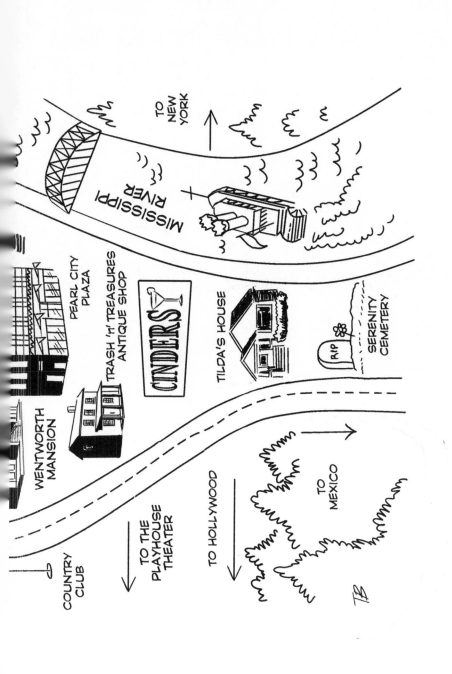

CHAPTER ONE:
IN WHICH VIVIAN FACES THE MUSIC AND BRANDY PLAYS SECOND FIDDLE

On this beautiful fall afternoon in Serenity — our small, picturesque town nestled on the banks of the Mississippi River — I would much rather have been doing almost anything else. This was, after all, Monday — the only day of the week that our antiques shop, Trash 'n' Treasures, is closed — and accompanying Mother to the courthouse on any day is not my idea of a good time.

But Vivian Borne (aka Mother) had been instructed to appear before the county commissioner to answer questions regarding some "unorthodox" actions she'd used a few weeks ago on her first case on the job as the newly elected sheriff of Serenity County.

Mother is in her midseventies, of Danish stock, widowed, bipolar, and quite attractive despite large, out-of-date eye-magnifying glasses. She is also a legendary local thespian, but an even more legendary local amateur sleuth, and a legend-in-the-making as our new county sheriff.

I am, by the way, Brandy Borne — thirty-three, blond by choice, a Prozac-popping prodigal daughter who post-divorce (my bad) crawled home from Chicago to live with Mother, seeking solitude and relaxation, but finding myself the frequent if reluctant accomplice in her mystery-solving escapades, now having to chauffeur her around in the sheriff's SUV, since she had lost her driver's license, and I don't mean the plastic I.D. card, which actually she still carries but which is stamped REVOKED.

(**Note to Brandy from Mother:** Dear, you seem to have lifted our personal profiles from the previous book, which was lifted from the one before that, which I believe is called plagiarism, and I would also advise you not to use such unwisely and unwieldy convoluted sentences.)

(**Note to Mother from Brandy:** Maybe I did plagiarize myself, but if so, I won't sue me. Besides, this time I added that you were sheriff and I was your driver.)

(**Note to Brandy from Mother:** Still, I think our profiles need freshening up.)

(**Editor to Vivian and Brandy:** Ladies . . . get on with it.)

Mother, riding figurative shotgun, was attired in a tan jumpsuit of her own design because the official shirt and pants were too scratchy and didn't stretch; I, behind the wheel, wore a rust-colored sweater, brown slacks, and beige suede booties, none of which were of my own design.

Right now she was saying, "I do hope Commissioner Gordon will go easy on me."

(Okay, Batman aficionados, snicker if you must, but that *is* his last name.)

I secretly hoped the commissioner would begin impeachment hearings, after what Mother had recently put me through during an Edgar Allan Poe festival in the hamlet of Antiqua (chronicled in *Antiques Ravin'*).

"Just tell the truth," I replied, as if I were rooting for her. I'm not (necessarily) a bad daughter, but I feared what kind of trouble she might get herself — all right, us — into. I mean, there was a literal shotgun in back and a stun gun on her duty belt.

Mother's head swiveled toward me. "Dear, I *always* tell the truth."

When I guffawed, she qualified her statement with, "Except about my age — which is no one's business but my own."

We had arrived downtown at the courthouse, where I found a parking spot in front.

As we exited the vehicle, Mother — carrying a large tote bag — said, "It's so nice be-

13

ing an official and not having to feed a meter anymore."

Actually, Mother had never fed a meter in her life — not with coins anyway. She bought cheap aluminum flat washers by the gross, by way of protesting The Man. Of course, now she was The Woman. . . .

The county courthouse, built in the 1880s, was a three-story edifice of Grecian grandeur whose cream-colored limestone bricks, columns, and clock tower reminded me of a big wedding cake, albeit a stale one. For years numbskulls (Mother's word, one of her favorites) had attempted to have the un-air-conditioned building torn down and replaced with a modern institutional monstrosity. But so far Mother and her friends at the Serenity Historical Preservation Society had managed to thwart any such efforts.

Personally, during the hot months of July and August, I avoided going in the place, where sweat-soaked clerks could be especially mean (ceiling fans can do only so much); and savvy criminal defense lawyers maneuvered to avoid trials being set during that time or else encounter crabby or nodding-off jurors, not to mention heat-stroked judges.

Entering the courthouse was like stepping

back in time — very little had changed, from the marbled flooring, walnut wainscoting, and pebbled-glass wooden doors to the old steam heat radiators. Even the light fixtures, converted from gas to electric, were at least a hundred years old. The only giveaway was the aluminum water fountains.

Gordon's office was on the first floor, just off the rotunda, and Mother and I went in through a door with COUNTY COMMISSIONER stenciled on the pebbled glass.

We could only take a few steps forward before running into the desk of the receptionist, an officious-looking middle-aged woman in a navy pantsuit, looking up from her computer screen with the enthusiasm of a longtime civil servant, which is what she was.

"Good afternoon, Sheriff Borne," she said brusquely.

I was not acknowledged. I was not an official deputy, after all. Mother said I was "ex-officio." I think that's Latin for "lackey."

The woman bent to the intercom speaker on the desk and pressed a button. "The sheriff is here."

"Send her in," a male voice responded gruffly.

Wow. Didn't *anybody* here like their job?

Mother went through the door into the

commissioner's inner sanctum, and I followed like her shadow.

Gordon's office was larger than the receptionist's, but not by much, and the furnishings were strictly perfunctory and almost old enough to interest the pair of antique sellers who had just entered. No waste of taxpayer's money here.

The commissioner cut an imposing figure behind the desk — even more so as he stood. Midforties, tall, with a crisply conservative haircut, neatly trimmed beard, and a tanned face thanks to summer weekends on the golf course.

"Sheriff Borne," he said, business-like.

"Commissioner Gordon," Mother replied respectfully.

(Okay that did strike me as amusing; maybe, when he needed her, he could summon her from the courthouse rooftop with a batty signal.)

The two nodded in lieu of shaking hands, then Mother took a chair in front of the desk, and he returned to his behind it. I found a seat behind Mother, next to the door.

Gordon opened his mouth to speak, but words didn't get the chance to emerge.

"How *is* your wife?" Mother asked. "I'm so pleased to hear that she's no longer hav-

16

ing to wear that horrible back brace."

His smile was small and almost sincere. "Amanda is doing fine. I'll tell her you inquired about her. Now, do you understand the purpose of this meeting?"

Mother smiled. "I believe you have some questions for me, which of course I'm delighted to answer, and how is the new grandbaby? First one, is it? You must be looking forward to your roles as doting grandparents!"

Mother was deluded if she thought this patter would soften him up.

"Yes, very much," Gordon said, somewhat impatiently. "And you understand, Sheriff Borne, that your answers, if insufficient or not to my liking, will warrant a formal hearing before the entire board of county supervisors."

"Well, doesn't that go without saying? As the submarine captain said, fire away!"

The commissioner breathed the first of many world-weary sighs as he consulted some papers on his desk. "According to the report you filed —"

"Pardon me," Mother interrupted. "But I suddenly sense a midafternoon drop in my blood sugar and I simply must have something to eat." She was reaching into the tote bag, drawing out a tin. "I brought along

17

some scones."

So that's what I smelled cooking in the middle of the night! I thought I'd dreamt it, since no baked goodies had been on offer for breakfast back at the Borne homestead.

Mother popped off the cover, then thrust the tin toward the commissioner. "Have one? I used *lots* of raisins. Big juicy ones!"

Gordon eyed the contents. "I do love raisins, but Amanda doesn't, and won't put them in anything she makes."

Mother always did her due diligence.

He went on, "But I'm afraid I can't accept, as delicious as they look. I react badly to gluten."

"Me too!" she exclaimed. "These scones are quite gluten-free."

Actually, Mother never met a gluten she didn't like.

"Well, in that case . . ." Gordon plucked out a plump scone.

Mother helped herself but didn't offer me one, knowing I sided with Amanda in the firm belief that cooked raisins are slimy. (Longtime readers expecting a gluten-free scone-with-raisins recipe at this point are out of luck, I'm afraid.)

Then — from out of the tote bag, like a rabbit from a hat — Mother produced a thermos. This was followed by two cups.

"Coffee?" Mother asked him.

"Why, uh . . . yes. Please."

She set the two cups on the edge of the desk and poured from the thermos. "I hope you like hazelnut."

"My favorite," he said.

Whodathunkit?

Mother handed the commissioner a cup, took the other, and sat back. "Now about these questions . . . ?"

Gordon chewed, brushing crumbs off of the papers, then swallowed.

(**Note to Reader from Brandy:** So as not to spoil our previous account, *Antiques Ravin',* for those who haven't read it — you will though, won't you? — some words in the following conversation have, at Mother's request, been redacted.)

"After reading the report you filed, Sheriff Borne," Gordon began sternly, "I'm concerned that you sometimes didn't follow law enforcement standards and protocol. In fact, in one instance, you actually broke the law."

"Might I suggest," Mother said sweetly, "we start with the smaller infractions and work our way up?"

Ignoring that, he went on. "According to your own words, you commandeered a **REDACTED**."

Mother shifted in her seat. "Perhaps 'commandeered' is too strong a verb — I'm afraid that was the wordsmith in me, embellishing a bit."

"Reports are to be strictly factual, Sheriff," Gordon advised. "But you *did* operate the **REDACTED**?"

"Yes, for about five miles, to the next crossing. But the **REDACTED** was sitting right there next to me — a nice young man named **REDACTED**. He even let me wear his hat and blow the whistle."

Gordon was making little notations in the margins of the report. "Let's move on. After Mr. **REDACTED** was **REDACTED**, you failed to notify the FBI. Why was that?"

"I had to be sure he really *had* been **REDACTED**. The FBI are very busy people — and getting busier every day! And as it turned out, they weren't needed after all. In fact, I did their work for them. Win-win!"

"Can you explain your actions to involve the **REDACTED** Indian Nation, which is *outside* your county jurisdiction?"

"Commissioner, if I hadn't, Mr. **REDACTED** would have died. The **REDACTED** Indian Nation was also instrumental in providing key information that led me to the killer."

"Information obtained at their casino,

where you admit you **REDACTED** while on duty."

Mother raised a finger. "One measly quarter! Which I found on the floor as I was going out and simply slipped into a slot. How was I to know I'd get lucky? Besides, I donated my entire winnings of **RE-DACTED**."

"And how did you get yourself *to* the **REDACTED**?" Gordon asked, his expression telegraphing he knew the answer.

"Yes, I admit I drove. I know that was technically wrong. But my poor ex-officio deputy here — my daughter, Brandy — was down with a migraine, and after all, there was a killer on the loose."

More note-taking, accompanied by another of those world-weary sighs.

"Any explanation for the destruction of private property," the commissioner said, "does not appear to be included in your report, Sheriff Borne."

"Oh?" Mother asked innocently. "I don't recall anything of that nature."

I piped up, "Three farm **REDACTED** and a **REDACTED** from Antiqua City Hall."

Mother said acidly over her shoulder, "Thank you, Deputy dear, for reminding me." Then back to Gordon: "Of course, I will *personally* pay for any and all damages. Anything else, Commissioner?"

He nodded gravely. "This is not concerning your report, Sheriff, but it has come to my attention that three cases of the soft drink **REDACTED** were sent to your office by the **REDACTED** Company of Atlanta. You should know that accepting *any* gift can be seen as a bribe."

He didn't realize a few scone crumbs remained in a corner of his mouth.

"Well, that *was* quite unexpected! How was I to know that the president of the **REDACTED** Company would so appreciate my suggestion of stocking their vending machines with **REDACTED** that he would instruct his minions to send me some! But in the future I will guard against such acts of appreciation and make sure any gifts are returned." Mother paused. "However, could you please overlook *this* gift, just this one time? **REDACTED** is so hard to come by, and half a case is gone."

The commissioner scratched his chin. "I didn't know they even still made that stuff," he said. "I used to be chubby in my teens, and lost a lot of weight drinking **REDACTED** — tasted terrible, but I got to really like it."

"I believe the formula was recently

changed from saccharin to NutraSweet —
which, to me, ruined the product — but
what I received was the *original* stuff."

The commissioner sat forward, tented his
hands, eyes wide. "Could you . . . Vivian, is
there any chance you could spare a case?"

"Of course! In fact, I'll have my deputy
send over some."

You may have figured out the drink in
question was TAB, and the company Coca-
Cola. I don't know why Mother insisted that
any of this be redacted.

I stood. "Commissioner Gordon" — and
I had to suppress a smile at the silly sound
of that — "if the only law the sheriff broke
was driving the SUV, can't something be
done to reinstate her license?"

"I don't see how," he replied. "Haven't
there been multiple vehicular charges?"

"Frankly," Mother said, "I've never understood why knocking over a mailbox should
lead to a county infraction. Shouldn't that
have been a federal matter?"

I said, "Commissioner, I will concede that
her infractions have infractions . . . but
couldn't she get a license to use a motorcycle?"

Gordon frowned. "That's an interesting
idea — the requirements *aren't* as restrictive
as a car." He looked at Mother. "But, in my

opinion, a police-grade motorcycle would be too hard for you to handle."

"How about a Vespa!" Mother exclaimed, clasping her hands in a childish "goody-goody" manner. "I've always wanted one ever since I saw Audrey Hepburn in *Roman Holiday*!"

But what I pictured was more like Toad in *American Graffiti*.

She was saying, eyes glittering, "It could be tricked out with siren and lights, in case I have to pull someone over! And be fitted with a big windshield to keep the bugs off my teeth."

The commissioner rubbed his forehead like maybe it was his turn to get a migraine. "I'll look into it."

Mother asked gingerly, "And will it be necessary for me to appear before the board?"

Gordon hesitated before answering. "I believe I can convince them that — after our talk — you fully understand where you went wrong, and will in the future adhere to a by-the-book work ethic. And it doesn't hurt that you *did* get results. We can't have some lunatic running around."

Mother frowned. "Well, I take issue with —"

I touched her sleeve. "He means the killer

24

we caught," I said.

"Oh. Well. That's different."

He thumped the report on his desk with a finger. "But make no mistake — you step out of line again, Sheriff Borne, and you'll find yourself impeached."

Mother beamed. "That has a nice ring to it!"

He blinked. "Impeachment?"

"No! 'Sheriff Borne.' And you may rest assured that I will henceforth stay in line with the precision of a Rockette!"

And she crossed her heart, with the fingers of her other hand crossed behind her back. Me, I was wondering if anybody else in history had ever before used both *Rockette* and *henceforth* in the same sentence.

He stood, releasing her, and one last sigh.

"Why don't I just leave this tin of scones," she said softly, conspiratorially. Then she packed the thermos and cups inside her tote bag, and we left.

Outside, in the cool autumn breeze, Mother paused on the portico of the courthouse. "Well, that went well. My research on the commissioner paid off! I didn't even have to use the A material."

"What would *that* have been?"

"Let's just say that what happens in Vegas doesn't necessarily stay in Vegas. I'll keep that one tucked away."

"Yeah, and you only had to bribe him twice."

Another first in the history of Mankind: a raisin scone and TAB bribe.

She breathed in deeply. "Will you just *look* at this *beautiful* day?"

"Where to now?"

"The Wentworth mansion."

"What? Why?"

"The owner wanted me to drop by and give him news about my meeting last night with the Historical Preservation Society. And while we're there, he can give us a tour. I've taken one, of course — more than one, actually — but never tire of it."

"That doesn't sound like official sheriff business."

She raised a forefinger. "Yours is not to reason why, dear, yours is but to do and drive."

So, with the sun continuing its slow decent in the clear blue sky, we headed to the SUV.

Soon we were cruising along Main Street, where the occasional law-abiding citizen gave us a wave, then we entered the trendy shopping block of Pearl City Plaza, with its antiques stores and boutiques and bistros. The end of the plaza signaled the conclusion of the downtown business section, and we began the slow-but-steady climb up West Hill. A few moderate homes sat at the base — our antiques shop was one — but as we ascended, the residences became bigger and better, increasing in grandeur, and value, commensurate with their view of the scenic Mississippi River.

At the top of the hill, where the land leveled out, was an impressive array of mansions, many built in the 1800s by city founders — lumbermen, bankers, and pearl button makers — exquisite examples of baroque, Queen Anne, Gothic Revival, Greek Renaissance, each a work of art determined to outshine the other.

I had been inside most of these mansions with Mother, who could usually wheedle an invitation from the owner — if not, she would find some pretext to drop by. But the Wentworth place I had seen only from the outside.

Mother was saying, "The first Benjamin Wentworth founded Wentworth Lumber Company, back in the eighteen seventies, which remained in business until a fire destroyed it several years ago, under the tutelage of Benjamin Wentworth the Third."

I recalled the incident, which happened just after I'd moved back in with her.

"People died, didn't they?"

"A night watchman and one firefighter. Tragic."

"What was the cause?"

"Undetermined," she said. "The whole place went up in minutes like a pile of —"

"Lumber?"

I pulled to the curb in front of a grand Queen Anne home, which sat back from the street on a small terrace. We exited the SUV, Mother gazing up at the place like a starving man at a sumptuous meal.

The three-story mansion was built of tan brick with a stone foundation, the roof consisting of multiple levels sporting several round turrets with their own conical roofs, offset by gables.

Steps, then a cement walk, took us to a wide porch that spanned the entire front of the house, whose numerous bay windows were fashioned of stained glass.

We approached a massive wooden door with beveled lead glass, where a round metal bell with a handle was set into the wood. Mother cranked the ancient bell, which then produced a loud ding on the other side.

After another crank of the bell, the door swung open to reveal a well-preserved silver-haired, middle-aged man with black-framed glasses, a straight nose, and prominent

28

dimpled chin. He wore a yellow sweater, tan slacks, and brown slip-on shoes.

"Hello, Vivian," he said warmly. "Or should I say Sheriff? Thank you for coming by."

"Hello, Jimmy," she practically purred.

Hmmm. Was I in the presence of yet another on the list of Vivian Borne's past paramours?

She glanced my way, gestured to our host. "Brandy, this is James Sutter, the owner. Jimmy, this is my deputy daughter."

I was really starting not to like that phrase — "Deputy Daughter" sounded like a cartoon show.

He held out a hand, which I shook. "Nice to meet you, Mr. Sutter."

"Of course, I know who *you* are," he said, his smile revealing white teeth that may or may not have been his. "And I'll call you Brandy and you call me Jimmy."

"Fine, Jimmy," I said, smiling back at him. "I've seen you driving Vivian around town — so, are you an official deputy?"

"No. It's more like involuntary servitude."

That got some nervous laughter out of Jimmy and an extremely strained smile from Mother.

"Well, come in, come in," he said.

We stepped through the portal.

As I said, I'd visited other grand homes on West Hill before, like the Blackwood, Butterworth, and Wright mansions — even the pseudo palace owned by Nastasya Petrova, who was distantly related to the Romanov dynasty — but what my eyes were about to discern was the crème de la crème of the Serenity mansion crop.

Mother was asking, "Could we impose upon you for a quick tour? Brandy's never been inside."

"Certainly," our host replied. "Only it will have to be limited to the downstairs. The upstairs rooms are being repainted and the plaster repaired, so the furniture is covered. But you can come back when it's all done."

We embarked upon the tour beginning with the dining room, Mr. Sutter histrionically narrating its many unique features, like the gleaming wood-paneled walls that led up to a beamed and coffered (sunken-paneled) ceiling, and the elaborately carved buffet with lion's heads, and matching custom-made table whose ten chairs were topped by the same lion's heads.

Also impressive was the bathroom with its floor-and-ceiling green glass tiles with black accents that Mrs. Benjamin Wentworth had spotted at the 1893 World's Fair in Chicago, and purchased for the then outlandish price of $18,000.

But probably the most beautiful — and reverent — spot in the mansion appeared to be the landing of the grand staircase, where — above a long velvet-padded seating bench — was a large, somewhat amateurish but charming portrait in oil of a child, blond and cherubic.

As I gazed up from the foot of the stairs, Mr. Sutter said solemnly, "Arabella was the Wentworths' only daughter, who died from scarlet fever at the age of five."

I said, more to myself than him, "Wealth can't protect people from tragedy."

Mother, who had been lurking within earshot, asked, "Jimmy, wasn't your late wife a Wentworth?"

Sutter turned toward her. "Shirttail relation. It was her idea to buy the mansion. Diane always fancied living here. Shall we move on to the kitchen?"

He led us back to a large kitchen that had retained the original black and white floor tiles with a very distinctive pattern. So distinctive, in fact, that I stood frozen in the doorway.

My eyes went questioningly to our tour guide.

"I know," Sutter said. "I always feel it necessary to point out that the house was built long before the Nazis incorporated the swastika motif. Actually, the double-hooked cross dates back to ancient Troy, where it meant 'good fortune.' "

Not such good fortune for either Hitler or the early Wentworths.

He went on, "But since the flooring is original to the house, it must remain."

I wasn't so sure. The rest of the kitchen had been changed, perhaps several times over, with modern appliances (although authentically pleasing). The cupboards might have been original, and certainly the oak table with high-backed caned chairs was of the period. All I knew was I couldn't ever eat in here.

After we had come full circle, returning to the entryway, I asked Mr. Sutter if all the furniture was his.

He chuckled. "Oh, no, I couldn't've afforded to buy *any* of it. Nearly everything belongs to the Wentworth estate, which stipulates that the antiques must remain with the house."

I was confused. "But you *do* own the house?"

He nodded. "That's right. I bought it from Ben Wentworth, who didn't want the responsibility of the place anymore — there was no restriction on the house itself, only that the contents remain with it."

"Doesn't that bother you?" I asked. "Not having your own things? Not being able to decorate the way you want?"

To me it would have been like living in a museum — no matter how valuable and handsome the contents, it was still . . . a museum.

He seemed surprised. "Not in the least, Brandy. Who wouldn't want to be around all this beauty?"

Maybe, if it was Art Deco.

I pressed: "But the responsibility . . ."

Sutter nodded. "That is true. But I enjoy the task." He paused. "Except . . . ever since Diane died, that task has become so much harder."

His eyes went to Mother, who was examining an unusual-looking vase on the center marble-topped round table. The vase was shaped like a nuclear reactor tower with a gold barber-pole-style band wrapped around midnight blue glass. But Sutter wasn't studying the antique, unless Mother qualified.

Holy cow! Was our host contemplating making Vivian Borne the new Mrs. Sutter? Didn't he know that Mother wouldn't be a caretaker to anyone else's things? And that included husbands.

She looked his way. "Is this an original Tiffany lava vase?"

"It is."

Her eyes, already huge behind the eyeglass lenses, got bigger. "I'd be afraid to dust it."

Not that she was big on dusting.

Sutter chuckled, then gestured toward the parlor. "Why don't we sit down for a while, and you can tell me how the board meeting went."

We followed our host through open pocket walnut doors into what I thought was the least impressive area of the downstairs — or maybe I'd just become jaded by all the splendor. But the very typically Victorian furnishings, however high quality, had none of the unexpected surprises of the dining room.

Mother and I sat on a curved velvet couch facing the fireplace, while Mr. Sutter took a needlepoint armchair, angled toward us.

"In a nutshell," Mother began (no comment), "the Historical Preservation Society believes we can get you another grant to help with the ongoing repairs."

He sighed in relief. "That would be wonderful. My only other option would be to put the house back on the market, and well, you know there was no interest last time."

"Yes," Mother said, nodding. "Not even

34

at the below-market price you'd asked."

Not many people want to buy a home that required them to be a museum curator.

Sutter shifted in his chair. "How . . . how much are we talking?"

Mother shrugged. "Hard to say. Grant dollars for historical homes are decreasing every year . . . but I think an amount of twenty thousand might be attainable."

Sutter looked disappointed, but only briefly. "That would certainly help with tuck-pointing the brick, which is especially needed on the side facing the river."

"I'll keep you informed," Mother said.

When the conversation between the pair turned borderline gossipy, I excused myself and went out into the anteroom, where a large elaborately carved grandfather clock was striking five. I walked over to the base of the staircase and stared up at the portrait of the little girl, who gazed back at me.

I hoped I'd never know the grief of losing a child.

Someone touched my arm, and I jumped a little.

"Time to go, dear," Mother said.

At the door I thanked Mr. Sutton for the tour, then went on out, while Mother stayed behind to exchange a few more words with him, in a way that verged on the intimate side. Jimmy Sutter seemed nice enough, but I couldn't see myself ever calling him Daddy.

After Mother finally joined me, and we were outside descending the steps, I said, "Tell me you're not interested in him."

"Dear, I *am* interested in him, just not seriously." She took my arm. "Don't worry, I have no desire to be the caretaker of anyone else's former belongings — furniture or otherwise."

Told you.

On the drive home, Mother couldn't stop chattering about the Tiffany lava vase, and how "Louie," the American artist and designer (and son of Charles Lewis Tiffany, founder of the Tiffany Company), had devised the unusual glass technique after a trip to Italy, where he was inspired by the volcanic eruption of Mount Etna in Sicily.

Frankly, I found the free-form abstract unattractive. But I'd take one. To sell.

At home — a two-story stucco white house with wide front porch — I pulled the SUV into the drive and up to a stand-alone one-car garage that was crammed full of Mother's garage/yard/dumpster finds.

Inside, we were greeted by the third member of our household — and arguably the smartest — Sushi, my brown-and-white diabetic shih tzu.

The little darling had her leash clenched in her tiny, sharp teeth, and I knew there'd be no putting her off. So I picked Sushi up, went outside, grabbed the plastic pooper-scooper (no plastic bag stooping for me), and off we went.

The evening was uneventful, and I was in bed with Sushi by ten, lights out.

Then I was being shaken awake by an hysterical Mother; the digital clock on the nightstand read 2:00 a.m.

"Wh-what?" I stuttered. "Is the house on fire?"

"Not *ours,*" she said, wild-eyed. "But the Wentworth mansion is in flames! Let's go!"

She was pulling my arm.

"But . . . I'm not dressed," I protested groggily.

Mother was — she'd taken to sleeping in one of her uniformed jumpsuits, in case she had to bail out of bed for a call to duty.

"Anyway, you're the sheriff," I said, grabbing a robe, "not the fire chief."

Which was the only thing that had stopped her from installing a fire pole.

On the way, she initiated the siren and lights in the SUV, even though it was the dead of night and the streets were deserted.

In the distance, the fire could be seen

lighting up the dark sky, and Mother urged me to drive faster as if we could do some good. She had no jurisdiction over a fire, which was first and foremost the fire department's job, and then the police department's, if something criminal had transpired.

But we were almost there.

Two fire trucks were in front of the mansion, along with two police cars and a paramedic truck, all blocking the street. I maneuvered the SUV as close as I could, and Mother jumped out before I'd even put the car into park.

She headed to the nearest yellow-suited fireman, who was grappling with a hose — another firefighter up in a bucket was aiming his at the roof's blazing turrets — and I hurried to catch up to her.

"Did Mr. Sutter get out?" she shouted at the hose grappler.

When the firefighter didn't seem to know, she moved on to find someone who might, and I stood watching the conflagration, thinking about the beautiful one-of-a-kind, priceless, irreplaceable antiques that made up the contents of the mansion, including the oil-painting portrait of the Wentworth's dead daughter, haunting if far less than priceless.

A female firefighter spun me around. "Your mother!"

"What about her?"

"I told her we couldn't reach Mr. Sutter without risking our lives, and she went inside!"

My jaw dropped, and I turned back to the house in time to see the roof collapse onto the second floor and the second floor onto the first.

A TRASH 'N' TREASURES TIP

When shopping for antiques online, it's best to buy from a respected, established dealer's website. But if you use eBay or other such sites, check the seller's reputation and feedback, then use your own judgment accordingly. And read the listings carefully. Before she got wise, Mother ordered an antique chair that turned out to be a miniature one for a dollhouse. No wonder she thought she'd gotten quite the bargain.

CHAPTER TWO:
IN WHICH VIVIAN
FLIES THE COOP AND
BRANDY CALLS FOUL

I watched in horror as the burning house toppled into itself in a cacophony of splintering wood, glass, brick, and mortar. Seconds crawled by, and I was chewing my fist, trying not to scream. Then, like a mirage out of the smoke, Mother staggered and collapsed onto the lawn, leaving fuming remains behind.

I ran toward her, but the female firefighter grabbed my arm and held me back. "Let the paramedics do their job," she said, firm but not unkind.

Even though I knew she was right, I still tried to wiggle out of the woman's grasp.

"They're her best chance now," she insisted, meaning the EMTs, and I stopped struggling.

I stood by helplessly as two paramedics bent over Mother — her clothes smoldering — making a quick assessment of her burns. Soon an oxygen mask was attached to her soot-smeared face, and they wrapped her in a silver blanket. Quickly but gently, she was placed on a gurney and delivered to the open doors of a waiting ambulance.

Then, with lights flashing, siren wailing, the vehicle disappeared into the night. Or was that morning?

I stood frozen in the heat. It had all happened so fast and yet, at the same time, in slow motion.

"Do you need a ride to the hospital?" the female firefighter asked, her face coming into focus.

"No, I . . . I have the sheriff's car."

"Are you sure you're up to driving?"

I nodded numbly, managed to mumble my thanks, and walked away.

At Serenity Hospital, despite my protestations, I was not allowed into the ER exam room to see Mother. Instead, I paced the emergency waiting room, alone, muttering to myself, my emotions swinging wildly from fury that she had taken such a stupid risk to fear that I might soon be without her, and back again.

The door to the ER hallway opened, and I stopped in my tracks, hoping, yet dreading, to see a doctor emerge with news.

But Tony walked in — our chief of police, and exactly the right person to give me

41

much-needed comfort. He was in his late forties with graying temples, steel-gray eyes, bulbous nose, square jaw, and just happened to be the big, strong man I was dating. Of course, right now he looked like someone who'd been dragged out of bed in the wee hours of the morning, which was the case.

"I just came from the fire," he said, coming to stand in front of me. "It's contained, but a complete loss of the house and its contents. . . . How is Vivian?"

I leaned against that barrel chest of his and let the tears finally flow.

After a while, he led me to a chair, then sat beside me.

I managed to speak. "I don't know anything yet."

Tony took my hand. "The doctors will do everything they can," he said, adding, "And the fact that they haven't air-lifted her to the burn center in Iowa City is a very good sign."

I suppose that should have made me feel better, but it did nothing to abate my anxiety. But his presence was reassuring in itself.

Sounding more like the police chief than my boyfriend, Tony was asking, "What were you doing there?"

I could almost hear the tacked-on "Ms. Borne."

I composed myself and told him about our visit yesterday to the Wentworth mansion regarding a grant the Historical Preservation Society might get to help Mr. Sutter with repairs. And when someone called our house with the news of the fire, Mother had insisted on going.

Frowning in concern, he asked, "So how did she get hurt?"

"Mr. Sutter was still inside."

Aghast, Tony said, "And she ran into a burning house to *save* him?"

My laugh was involuntary. "I *know*!"

Tony shook his head slowly, then sighed his response: "Vivian has done more than her share of bone-headed things in her time, but . . . sorry."

"No apology necessary." I shrugged a shoulder. "All I can figure is that she may've had a previous history with Mr. Sutter that prompted her to action . . . if you get my drift."

He did. He knew of Mother's youthful indiscretions. And some not so youthful ones too.

Even so, I had trouble swallowing just how big, and ridiculous, a risk she had taken. Mother placed Mother above everyone else and was not generally inclined to self-sacrifice.

The door to the ER's inner sanctum opened and a male doctor in a white coat approached, his expression unreadable. I recognized him as the Eastern Indian physician who had once treated me here, after Mother accidently tased me (*Antiques Frame*).

"You're Mrs. Borne's daughter?" he asked, apparently not remembering me. "Brandy, is it?"

I nodded and stood, knees wobbly.

He said matter-of-factly, "Your mother has sustained second-degree burns on her arms and legs, and —"

I interrupted. "Will she have to be taken to the burn unit?"

"No."

As relief swept over me, the doctor went on. "The injuries aren't life-threatening, but she did inhale a good deal of smoke, and for that reason I'd like her to stay overnight."

"Can I see her?" I asked.

"She's having a lung X-ray right now," he replied. "I suggest you go home and come back in the morning."

Then, apparently not having a smile to spare, he went back the way he came.

When I hadn't moved, Tony touched my arm. "She'll be just fine. And so will you, after a little sleep."

I nodded my agreement.

Tony said, "Come on . . . I'll follow you home."

He was well aware I wasn't supposed to drive the sheriff's vehicle without Mother present.

We left through the ER entrance into the still of a starry night, the chilly autumn air feeling like a cool drink of water.

When we'd reached the SUV, Tony said, "Brandy, this may not be the best time to get into this . . ."

No, it wasn't! Whatever "this" was.

I turned to him, weary and wary.

"Try to keep Vivian out of the fire investigation," he said. "That's the job of local and state authorities."

"Well, she *is* the sheriff."

"Yes, but if their conclusion points to arson, then that puts the matter on my patch."

My stare caused him to raise a protective palm.

He added, "I'm just anticipating a potential problem."

I said wryly, "We know two things. First, no one can anticipate what Mother will do.

45

And second, there *will* be a problem."

He grinned. "And third, maybe the sun will rise and set. Just see what you can do, Brandy. That's all I ask."

I poked his chest with a finger. "Okay, but don't put this all on me. If she *does* get out of hand, you'll have to rein her in."

"Will do. Unless the bronco bucks me off."

As he turned toward his vehicle parked a few spots away, I touched his arm. "Tony . . . thanks for coming."

He shrugged. "It's my job."

"No. You were concerned. About me *and* Mother. That means a lot."

He gave me a nod, paused as if considering whether to give me a kiss, and instead threw me a smile.

We got into our respective vehicles, and he trailed me home. We exchanged waves as I pulled into the drive.

Inside the two-story stucco white house with its wraparound porch, Sushi was waiting in the entryway. I scooped her up with every intention of trudging upstairs to bed, but I made it only as far as the Victorian couch, where I flopped on my side, the little darling curled up beside me.

I awoke about four hours later with a kink

in my neck and figured the only way to work it out was to get up and moving, so I might as well head back to the hospital and see how Mother was faring. I fed Sushi, put her out, and then resisted her urgings to accompany me, since most hospitals aren't big on furball visitors.

I arrived around eight-thirty, arms laden with a cardboard tray of two vanilla lattes and pumpkin cake donuts, plus a bag of clothes for Mother, including another of her sheriff's jump suits.

In the hallway leading to her room, I encountered her second-in-command, Deputy Charles Chen, crisply attired in pressed tan uniform. He'd just departed her chamber and seemed vaguely amused.

This played into the slight irritation I felt, knowing he'd seen her before I had.

"How is she?" I asked.

In his late thirties, Deputy Chen had an interesting background. In 1980, to improve American–Chinese relations, Serenity had begun a sister/city program, adopting a town in China — Hebi — that was relatively the same size as ours. Our mayor and city council members invited a delegation of Hebi's citizens to visit our town, to be squired around and learn about local farming.

Chen's parents, who were part of that delegation, fell in love with Serenity and never returned home. Charles was born a year later, and his parents eventually became U.S. citizens.

With a little laugh, the deputy said, "Nothing can keep that woman down. She's already holding court in there!"

"I'm not surprised. Anyone in particular, or just entertaining the nurses?"

"Oh, it's that woman from the Historical Preservation Society."

"Mrs. Snydacker?"

He gave me half a grin. "That's the one. Just don't ask me to pronounce it."

I leaned in a little. "Listen, uh, Deputy . . . I really appreciate everything you do for Mother. Must not be much like working for Sheriff Rudder."

His eyebrows went up. "Well, every day is a new adventure!"

"Tell me about it. Anyway, I'm grateful to you."

He gave me a little embarrassed smile, and a salute. "Bye, Brandy — I've got a full day ahead of me."

"Good luck," I said.

And off he went.

I had wanted to spend time alone with Mother before the well-wishers and gossips descended, to vent my unhappiness with her (now that I knew she'd be okay), but that would have to wait.

She was cranked up in bed beneath the thin covers in her private room, wearing one of those dreadful hospital gowns. Her left forearm was bandaged, and her right hand had been stuck with an IV. An oxygen tube snaked up into her nose.

Upon spotting me, Mother said hyper-cheerfully, "Ah! Brandy! You know Evelyn Snydacker."

Well, her painkiller must be working, anyway, I thought.

The midfifties smartly dressed, red-haired Mrs. Snydacker — proud owner of one-too-many face-lifts — had recently traded her position as president of the League of Women Voters for the Historical Preservation Society post.

I nodded at the woman, who was at Mother's bedside, taking up the only chair, which she did not vacate for me. She did offer me a patronizing smile.

Mrs. Snydacker said, "Your brave mother was just about to tell me of her valiant effort to save poor Mr. Sutter."

Either that or how my valiant mother made a brave effort to save poor Mr. Sutter.

Mother, eyeing my tray, asked eagerly, "Is

that for me, darling girl? They're *late* with breakfast."

"Glad to see your appetite is doing well." I dropped the bag of clothes on a small counter, then handed her a Styrofoam cup of latte and a donut.

Mother took a sip from the lid. "Yummy. Skim milk, I hope."

"Oh, yes." It wasn't, but why bother having a latte at all if it doesn't contain at least whole or two percent?

Mrs. Snydacker prompted, "Please continue, Vivian, and don't stint on the details."

Mother never stinted on a detail, or anything else, really.

"Well, if you insist," Mother replied, hauling herself up straighter in the bed. "Anywho, there I was, on the sidewalk, watching that *magnificent* building going up in flames, when someone said that Jimmy was still inside!" She interrupted her melodramatic reading with a chomp on the donut. She chewed. Swallowed. "Pumpkin! My favorite."

We waited.

"Well!" she continued, with the enthusiasm of a gossip getting ready to share the dirt, "I couldn't simply stand by and not do my best to mount a rescue — Jimmy and I were old friends, after all."

Friends? Is that what she called it?

"So I ran to the front door," she went on, "despite the billowing smoke, then turned my head and took a deep breath — I used to be on the high school swim team, you know, and could swim underwater for over three minutes — and inside I went!"

And another bite of donut went inside her.

"I rushed toward the grand staircase — it was like something out of *Titanic,* only fire not water — and was about to start up when the flames came rushing down at me . . . the stairs completely engulfed in flames! It was as if Dante's Inferno itself was manifesting to swallow me up!"

She swallowed up a sip of latte.

Frowning, she asked me, "Are you quite *sure* this is skim? Where was I?"

I said, "About to get swallowed by Dante's Inferno."

"Ah, yes. So. I had run out of breath . . ."

A rare occurrence.

". . . and, rather than gulp in any foul smoky air, I held my breath just a little longer and sidestepped falling beams and burning furniture, navigating a veritable fiery obstacle course, until I was able to make it back outside."

Without Jimmy Sutton. Something smelled and not of smoke.

"And that, my dears, is the last I remember until waking up in the ER, as if from a terrible, overwrought nightmare."

Yeah. Knew the feeling.

Meanwhile, the final bite of donut disappeared into her mouth.

"A *remarkable* tale." Mrs. Snydacker sighed. "Like something out of Edgar Allan Poe!"

I braced myself, fearful Mother might begin her famous recitation of "The Raven." Make that infamous.

Her guest was saying, "You really should receive a medal of valor."

Mother demurred. "That might be saying too much, Evelyn. I didn't actually save Jimmy." She paused. "But a citation for bravery *would* be nice. I'm sure the sheriff's department has such a thing, and perhaps the fire department does as well."

Mrs. Snydacker rose. "Well. I will be sure to mention it to the mayor."

"Thank you, dear."

"But for now, I must be going. I've an appointment at nine with a reporter from the *Sentinel* who wants to do a story about the tragic loss of the Wentworth mansion."

"How nice for you," Mother said. Which I thought was gracious of her until she added, "And should the reporter wish to interview

52

me, I will not be hard to find, for the nonce."

For the nonsense, too.

"I'll mention that," the woman replied.

When Mrs. Snydacker had gone, I moved to the empty chair. "I thought you wanted nothing to do with the *Sentinel.*"

This dated back to when their theater critic (who also handled obituaries and farm news) had given Mother a lackluster review of her one-woman performance of Libby Wolfson's *I'm Takin' My Own Head, Screwin' It on Right, and No Guy's Gonna Tell Me That It Ain't.*

Mother tossed a casual hand. "Well, dear, I've always said let bygones be bygones."

"Oh? When exactly was that?"

She frowned and looked at me as if noticing my presence for the first time. "Now, Brandy, if you've come to belittle me, in my time of need . . ."

I frowned back at her. "I've come to ask you what the h-e-double-hockey-sticks you were doing running into that burning house! You could've been killed. Didn't you even think of *me*?"

"Well, that's rather a selfish outlook, dear."

There was a knock on the doorjamb.

"Hope I'm not intruding," Miguel Ricardo said, then stepped into the room. Miguel, in his midthirties with dark wavy hair and an

53

athletic build, was the stage manager at the Playhouse Theater.

Despite his rather obvious charms, Miguel and Mother were not exactly simpatico, although they put on a good front, each needing the other. But she was firmly convinced that the stage manager lusted after her job as the theater's artistic director.

Mother all but purred, "You're not intruding at all, my dear boy."

I suspected she was glad for the interruption.

The stage manager came forward. "I heard what happened, just terrible, and thought this might cheer you up." From behind his back, he produced a bouquet of flowers wrapped in clear plastic, like a magician performing an easy but nonetheless surprising trick.

"Oh, you darling boy!" Mother cooed, accepting the gift. "How very thoughtful of you." She took an exaggerated sniff, then passed the bouquet to me. "Find something to put these in, would you, dear?"

A bedpan, maybe?

I stood and went into the bathroom, where I indeed found a plastic bedpan, filled it with water, lay the flowers in it so that

54

their stems were covered, and returned with it.

Miguel looked taken aback as I placed the arrangement on the wide windowsill, but Mother seemed pleased, saying, "Very nice, dear. Excellent thinking outside the box!"

Or within the pan.

I was no competition for Mother in such things, of course. Once, during a manic repurposing phase at home, she filled an old enamel bedpan with floating candles and used it as a dining room table center-piece.

Like Mrs. Snydacker, Miguel — who had confiscated my chair, as I'd been on my feet raving and ranting at the patient — wanted to hear all of the details relating to Mother's rescue attempt. In this version, she made it halfway up the burning staircase before it began to collapse, and she had to leap off, else be swallowed by flames.

"Very noble," Miguel said, "but foolish."

"Thank you."

"We would not want to lose you, Vivian. You know, I'd been working at the mansion myself, painting the upper-floor rooms. The place was something of a firetrap."

Nodding, Mother said, "I knew someone was doing that kind of work there. I didn't realize it was you."

He shrugged. "Have to bring in some extra money when we're between productions at the Playhouse." A sigh. "I suppose now I'll have to deal with Sutter's estate to get paid. Several hundred dollars' worth of my painting supplies went up in smoke! Good thing I kept the receipts."

"I'm sure you'll come out all right," she said, which would sound sincere to most people, but not to me.

The stage manager shifted in the chair. "If there's anything I can do for you, Vivian, while you're recuperating, do please let me know." Which also sounded sincere, but not to me.

"There's nothing I can think of," Mother replied pleasantly, "but if I come up with something, I'll let you know."

That I believed.

Miguel cleared his throat, and I figured he was about to get around to the real reason for the visit, since Mother's welfare was probably not it.

"As you know, the tryouts for the new play are tomorrow night," he said, "and seeing as how you're in the hospital, I'd be happy to step in."

I looked at Mother, knowing that he'd *already* stepped in . . . it.

"No need," she chirped. "I'll be there with

bells on."

He eyed her bandaged arm. "Are you sure?"

"Tut tut. This is merely a superficial wound — a flesh wound, as they used to say in the old westerns. Nothing worse than one might get from a hot stove."

A hot stove in a burning house with the grand stairway engulfed in flames.

She went on: "Your concern is *most* heart-warming, but not, I assure you, necessary. And thank you for the flowers. Rarely has a bedpan been graced with such beauty."

Dis-missed!

The stage manager stood, smiled wanly, nodded, then strode out.

"The snake!" Mother muttered. "Why, he can just *smell* the directorship!"

"Maybe it's just the smoke."

Something had been bothering me about her various varying recitations of heroism, something that went beyond her usual embellishments. Mother was downright fibbing.

I moved to her bedside. "You weren't really trying to save Mr. Sutter, were you? You may be fond of your old flames, but none of them are worth burning over. Are they?"

Her eyes avoided mine.

"*Are* they?"

She looked at me languidly. "No, dear. Memories last forever, but old loves fade away. Anyway, I'm neither that brave nor foolish."

I felt my chin crinkle as my face drew in upon itself. "It was that ugly Tiffany *vase* you wanted to save! *Wasn't* it?"

"No comment."

My frown softened into a quizzical look. "But you didn't come *out* with it."

"That's certainly true."

"Why?"

"Well, the truth is the truth, isn't it?"

"That's rich, coming from you. Quit dodging. Why didn't you save the life of that vase?"

"Simple. Because it wasn't there, dear."

"Where is it, then?"

"Now *that's* an excellent question. Get me the gauze and tape in that drawer." She gestured impatiently toward the nightstand.

"What for?"

"Must you question everything?"

If I didn't, I'd really be in trouble. But I carried out her orders nonetheless, placing the requested items in her outstretched palm.

Mother made a thick square from the gauze, tore off a stretch of tape, then reached for the clamp on the IV tube.

Alarmed, I asked, "What are you doing?"

"What does it look like? Shutting off the drip."

"Why?"

"Because I'm getting out of here."

"But you haven't been released!"

"I'm releasing myself on my own recognizance."

She clamped the drip, placed the gauze over where the IV entered her skin, then pulled the needle out. She needed my help in affixing the tape over the gauze, which I did, even as I threatened to call the nurse.

"Don't you dare!" she snapped, and threw back the covers, revealing legs that were splotched with red here and there, and shiny with ointment, but were not bad enough to require bandaging.

Mother got out of the bed and stood before me. "I've got something of vital importance to do, and time is of the essence. Now, go watch the hallway while I get dressed, and we'll go when the coast is clear."

She snatched up the bag of clothes and disappeared into the bathroom.

Around noon, I steered the SUV into a parking spot in front of the courthouse. On the way, Mother had been tight-lipped, other than giving me my marching orders. We exited the vehicle, went up a few cement steps, then followed the long sidewalk that cut through an expansive manicured lawn dotted with ancient oak trees and beds of colorful autumn mums to where double glass doors awaited.

Our destination turned out to be the office of the coroner, one of about a dozen small rooms on the second floor, encircling the upper rotunda occupied by various city officials.

Mother approached a wood and pebble-glassed door that read HECTOR HORNSBY, COUNTY CORONER, and without knocking, she — we — barged in.

The coroner's office was even smaller than the commissioner's. No secretary at the gate, just Hector behind a metal desk — a middle-aged, round, balding, round-faced, bespectacled man who appeared deer-in-the-headlights startled upon seeing her.

"Oh," he said. "You've been released from the hospital, I see."

Behind Mother, I said, "More like escaped."

Hector asked, "Something you want, Vivian — er, Sheriff?"

"Yes. An autopsy performed on James

60

Sutter. Toot sweet."

Hector's eyes bulged behind the spectacles. "Whatever for?"

Her chin lifted. "I suspect foul play."

He sat back, the chair creaking, then folded his arms and rested them on a protruding paunch. "On what evidence?"

"For the moment, I'd rather not say."

His frown, on that round face, had a pasted-on look. "Sheriff, I can't spend the taxpayer's money without a valid reason for the autopsy. As you well know, James Sutter's death was due to the fire."

Mother closed in on the desk. "He was examined?"

"No need. I've seen countless deaths by fire."

"I see. Let's not *count* this one out just yet. What if, because of your negligence, someone gets away with murder? That would be dereliction of duty."

The chair snapped forward. "Are you questioning my competence?"

"I merely think it would be prudent to have the medical examiner look at the body. It would be terrible to end so stellar a career on an oversight." She paused, adding, "Especially when you're up for reelection this year."

Hector regarded her with silent hostility,

61

then opened a drawer, withdrew a paper, and slapped it on the desk.

"All right," he said. "I'll authorize your autopsy." It sounded like he really did mean *her* autopsy. He picked up a pen. "But if the medical examiner doesn't find anything to back up your claim, yours will be the authority I cite!" He waggled the pen at her. "And you'll be up for reelection sometime too."

"Where *is* Jimmy?" Mother asked. "In the hospital morgue?"

Hector began filling out the form. "Neither. His stepson, Gavin Sutter, had him transported to the funeral home." He paused to give Mother a smug little smile. "I believe the body was to be cremated. You may want to hurry."

The aptly named Dunn Cremation and Burial, a modern facility on the edge of town, had put Serenity's other long-standing funeral home out of business, as more and more folks opted for "ashes to ashes, dust to dust."

But not Mother. She wanted to be coifed and adorned, laid out for display in a white coffin wearing a dress she'd already picked out and designated in her closet, and intending to be interred in a crypt she'd purchased in the big above-ground marble mausoleum along with Serenity's highest society.

Mother ordered me to drive around to the back of the facility and park by the awninged entrance where the deceased were discreetly delivered.

As per usual, Mother jumped out before I'd shut off the engine, and hurried inside, in a way few customers here did.

I followed, catching up to her at a door labeled CREMATORIUM, which she flung open wide. I followed tentatively.

The room was all white and stainless steel. Straight ahead was a roller belt and on it a mahogany casket moved inextricably toward a yawning chamber, whose mouth danced with hungry flames.

Mother shouted, "Stop the presses!"

The funeral owner, Mr. Dunn — impeccably dressed in a dark gray pin-striped suit, his white hair parted on one side and perfect — was standing at the controls watching the procedure. Startled, he turned to her.

"Is that James Sutter?" Mother bellowed.

"Yes. . . . What — ?"

Striding toward him, she commanded, "As sheriff of Serenity County, I order you to halt the procedure."

Visibly rattled, Dunn nevertheless did as

he was told, turning back to the controls, preventing the coffin from meeting the waiting flames.

Off to the side was a glassed-in observation room reserved for relatives of the deceased to view the procedure if they wished. Inside stood three people: a man and woman, both about forty, and a younger version of the woman, perhaps twenty.

The man flew out of the room and descended upon Mother like an avenging angel.

A six-footer with short-cropped sandy-colored hair, he had an angular face that may or may not have been handsome — I couldn't tell, because it was contorted with anger. He wore a gray suit and black tie.

He demanded, "What in God's name are you doing?"

She regarded him coolly. "Nothing in God's name. What I'm doing is in the name of the law. I'm stopping this cremation."

"Why?"

"You're Jimmy's stepson?"

He looked at her in dazed confusion. "Yes. Gavin Sutter."

"Well, I'm Sheriff Vivian Borne, and I've ordered an autopsy."

"You have to be joking!"

"I never joke."

She doesn't. Really. No sense of humor whatsoever. You laugh at her, not with her.

Mother was saying, "I have good reason to believe your stepfather was murdered."

She climbed way out on that limb. And me without a saw.

"That's insane!" Gavin said. He turned to Dunn, looking for help or perhaps a ray of sanity. "Can she *do* this?"

The funeral owner shrugged. "This kind of thing doesn't come up that often."

Gavin rotated back to Mother. "Well, as next of kin I *won't* give my consent."

"Your consent isn't necessary," Mother told him, producing the paper given to her by Hector. To Dunn she said, "Please transport Mr. Sutter to the hospital morgue."

Mother turned abruptly and left, me trailing after her.

In the SUV, I said, "You could have handled Gavin with a trifle more compassion, you know."

"I suppose," she allowed. "But I prefer to apologize later . . . *if* I can eliminate him as a suspect."

A TRASH 'N' TREASURES TIP

To protect your identity and money, look for secure payment options such as Auction

65

Payment Network (APN) and PayPal, or places that have current fraud protection software to ensure only trustworthy sellers. I thought a website that offered a bargain-priced Chanel bag was legit, but it wasn't — the site *or* the bag, which I still have (please don't rat me out).

CHAPTER THREE:
IN WHICH VIVIAN FLAMES OUT AND BRANDY GETS BURNED

Dearest ones!

This is Sheriff Vivian Borne taking over the narrative because Brandy is simply too squeamish to accompany me to the late Jimmy's autopsy.

But *you* aren't, are you? You're certainly curious about what a medical examiner can possibly discern from a burned body.

Me too!

But lest you worry, let me assure you this won't be visually graphic like some episodes of *CSI* or *Criminal Minds,* or even the mild-mannered *Murdoch Mysteries* series. Of course, the printed word often can conjure up disturbing images in one's mind that outdo more literal depictions on screen — just consider of the works of Edgar Allan Poe. "The Tell-Tale Heart" can still make me shiver! *Buh-bump-buh-bump-buh-bump . . .*

Uh-oh . . . I can sense that a few faint-oftelltale-heart readers may be on the verge of bailing — well, no harm, no foul! I won't think any less of you, even though Jimmy himself is well beyond *buh-bumping* at this stage of things. Just pick up the story line with the paragraph beginning, "Dear Reader."

All others who wish to be enlightened, ye of stout tell-tale hearts, come along.

(**Note to Vivian from Editor:** Are you sure this is a good idea?)

(**Note to Editor from Vivian:** I gave readers a "skip to," didn't I? Options are always a positive!)

(**Note to Vivian from Editor:** All right, but keep it clinical — no gore!)

(**Note to Editor from Vivian:** Roger Wilco. No gore, as the Supreme Court once said.)

The autopsy room, in the lower reaches of the hospital (isn't that more dignified than saying "bowels"?), was similar to a regular operating room except that it contained different procedural apparatus, and coolers for the bodies.

Jimmy was stretched out on his back on a stainless-steel examination table that had a perforated top for the drainage system, plus a small sink with faucets at one end. His badly burned body was black, purple, and gray, the flesh peeled back like the bark of a birch tree, his face nearly indistinguishable. A strip of white cloth discreetly covered his lower abdomen, possibly for my benefit.

Tom Peak was the medical examiner, a tall middle-aged man with salt-and-pepper hair and a long, lined face. He had on a white smock with lapel microphone, blue latex gloves, and plastic goggles.

I stood next to him on one side of the table, sans white smock but wearing the protective goggles that just barely fit over my own glasses.

He said, "No interruptions, or you're out."

"I'll be as quiet as a church mouse," I replied. Then, recalling that my church sometimes had some pretty noisy meeses, I added, "I won't make a peep."

Which implied I planned to be quiet as a baby bird, and they aren't really quiet at all, but . . .

"See that you don't."

Tom tapped the little microphone, gave his name, the date, and the location of the autopsy; then, consulting a clipboard with a printout, he continued, "The subject is James Sutter . . . male . . . length seventy-two inches . . . weight, one hundred ninety-six pounds . . ."

"Oh, he was heavier than that," I said, and

immediately clamped both hands over my mouth, like one of the three famous see-no-hear-no-speak-no monkeys.

Tom glared at me, and I made a "zip" sign across my lips.

His attention returned to Jimmy and the microphone. "I will be conducting an external examination —"

"Just *external*?" I blurted.

Tom covered the mic with a latexed hand. "Vivian, I warned you!"

"But . . . then you'll proceed to an *internal* exam, correct?"

"The external will determine whether an internal is warranted. Now, no more interruptions. *Please.*"

Unhappy, I nodded.

Tom continued with his evaluation. "The subject has been badly burned over ninety percent of his body."

He lifted the head and turned it slowly to one side and then the other. "There appears to be trauma to the back of the skull."

"Goodie!" I exclaimed. "Now you'll *have* to do the internal."

He thrust an arm with pointing finger toward the door. "Out! Oh-you-tee!"

Not taking this literally, I commented, "You'll have to take a biopsy of the lungs and esophagus for traces of smoke inhalation."

"Leave!"

Apparently it *was* literal. I started out, saying over my shoulder, "And if there *isn't* any, Jimmy was killed before the fire."

"Thank you for that final insight, Sheriff."

"I'm going . . . I'm going. . . ."

I went, but in a most self-satisfied fashion.

Dear reader, I am so terribly sorry that we got thrown out of the autopsy room. (My first time, too!) (Not my first time getting thrown out of somewhere, of course.) But I'm sure in time another such procedure will come along, and I will keep you in mind.

Nevertheless, I have created a problem for myself. Which is, what am I going to write for the rest of this chapter? I certainly don't want to bounce the ball back to Brandy (alliteration is fun!), so I'll tell you something that has really gotten my dander up lately.

Normally, I would not talk about politics for fear of alienating readers, but since both the right and the left have been equally offensive in this matter, I feel compelled to rectify it.

What is "it?"

"It" is cable news guests and anchors referring to those who are judged to be (by one side or the other) "bad actors," which is an insult to those of us who toil so nobly in the theatrical community. This abominable phrase is giving bad actors everywhere a bad name! Even worse is the usage of "bad-faith actors," which is doubly offensive, mixing religion with politics, *and* with the thespian arts.

So I say to politicians (and news commentators), stick to your own profession and stay out of others! You both have plenty of "bad" in your own backyards!

Brandy back.

Boy, that was quick for Mother. She's had half chapters before, but that was, what? A fifth of one? Maybe, considering the autopsy subject matter, you should have stuck with me — but not that much is happening on my end.

Having no stomach for attending the examination of a badly burned cadaver, I dropped Mother at the hospital, then (technically doing so illegally) drove the sheriff's car the short distance home, parking it in front of the house.

Mother had assured me that when the postmortem procedure was done, she'd finagle a ride to her office downtown at the new county jail, so I didn't expect to see her for some time.

Inside, I put Sushi outside, then had a quick lunch, retrieved Sushi, then took her with me to the C-Max, which was parked in the drive.

I was looking forward to spending a quiet afternoon at our much-neglected antiques shop, Trash 'n' Treasures, which we (sort of) maintained in a house we owned at the end of the downtown shopping district in a residential area just before the climb up West Hill.

Ever since Mother became sheriff and I became her chauffeur, we had been terribly spotty about our shop hours. So Mother devised a plan of letting customers know when we were open, an idea she'd gotten from a BBC news report that said whenever the Queen was in residence at Buckingham Palace, the Royal Standard flag was flying. You know where this is headed.

Mother had a pole installed off the porch, where we could simultaneously display any combination of four pennant-style flags with different letters — V for Vivian, B for Brandy, S for Sushi, and J for Joe, my ex–U.S. Marine friend who sometimes helped out in a pinch. No flags meant we weren't open, of course. But sometimes, when we were really busy, all four would be flapping in the wind.

Mother's nutty idea actually worked pretty well. Folks could see from a distance if anyone was in, and who it was, without trudging up to the door only to be greeted by a hand-scrawled "Closed" sign.

Plus, we quickly discovered that when Queen Mother was in residence (usually Sundays) we had the most business, especially from her gossipy friends as well as tourists who remember us from our short-lived reality TV show. I rated next, as costar, and then Joe, who could be off-putting to some by his PTSD syndrome (he'd been in Iraq). Sushi's flying flag boosted everyone's ratings.

So, after unlocking the door and turning off the alarm, I retrieved my flag and Sushi's and went out to raise them on the pole.

Back inside, the next thing I did was to go into our working, well-stocked 1950s kitchen to make a pot of coffee and some chocolate chip cookies for the customers and me (but mostly me).

While everything else in the kitchen was for sale, two items were not: the green Norge refrigerator with a little clock in its door, and the white GE Stratoliner that looked as if a jukebox had gotten busy with a stove. Those appliances would be a pain to replace if snapped up — unless the price offered was one we couldn't refuse.

Anyway, with the coffeepot percolating and the cookies baking, I sat on a chrome chair with red vinyl upholstery at the table with its laminated boomerang print, and considered just what I needed to accomplish this afternoon.

Not only was the kitchen a working one, the other rooms showcased appropriately placed antiques and collectibles — couches, end tables, floor lamps, wall paintings, and nicknacks in the living room; formal table and chairs, sideboard, china cabinet (stocked) in the dining room; and you get the idea. The upstairs hall closet was even stocked with vintage towels and bedsheets and blankets. The basement contained tools and "man-tiques," like beer signs and sports memorabilia, plus the attic held steamer trunks, old doors, and orphaned chairs. You could move right in.

And right now it looked like someone had — only they hadn't cleaned up after themselves. Looking around, with a forefinger to one cheek, I could see the obvious: The entire house could use dusting and straightening.

But first I needed sustenance. The built-in timer on the stove dinged, and my kitchenmitted hand pulled out the tray of steaming cookies. Not waiting for them to cool, I transferred the gooey confections onto an oval Fire King jade platter, which I placed on the table, reserving several for myself on a smaller plate. Then I poured coffee into a thick-rimmed green Fire King mug, added some milk, and took my bounty out to the small checkout counter installed in the entryway of the house.

There, I got up on a stool and turned on the computer. Sushi was in her little leopard-print bed on the floor behind me, resting, but waiting for a little piece of a cookie that didn't have chocolate (bad for dogs) to be dropped accidently on purpose.

Making an executive decision that the dusting and straightening could wait till later, I began to search the internet for Tiffany lava vases, such an item being on my mind because of the Wentworth one that Mother had failed to rescue. I wanted to see what was out there, what they were worth, and if any were for sale.

One hour, four cookies, and two cups of coffee later (during which time there wasn't a single customer, regardless of Sushi's flag flying), I'd found five lava vases at various museums (photos, no values given), three at art galleries (photos, price upon request), one at an auction site where it had sold six months ago for $75,000 (woah!), and zip on eBay.

While all these vases were decorated with gold on a black or midnight blue background, each was distinctly different from the others in design: gold dripping down from the rim like thick frosting on the sides of a cake; or splotched like a one-color Pollock painting; or mixed into the dark background paint, like swirling cinnamon sugar into coffee cake batter with a knife.

Yes, I was still hungry, despite the cookies. Why do you ask?

My least favorite pattern was an unappetizing one — random gold blobs that made the vase look as if it were covered in blisters, or maybe had a bad case of smallpox. (Louie, what *had* you been thinking?)

But none of these had the barber-pole-style design like the one I'd seen at the Wentworth mansion.

I looked away from the computer as the front door opened, and a woman about my age entered, plump and plain, with short mousy-brown hair, and wearing a navy pants suit.

"Hello, Brandy," she said, bounding toward me with a big smile.

". . . Hello."

The woman looked familiar, but I couldn't place her.

"How *are* you?" she asked.

"Fine. Just fine."

Sushi, roused from her bed, came around the counter with tail wagging and got up on her hind legs to paw at the lady's pants.

"Well, hi, Sushi," my visitor (customer?) said, bending to pet the dog's head.

Who was this woman who seemed to know us? Then it hit me: Gladys Gooch, the manager of the bank in the tiny town of nearby Antiqua (*Antiques Ravin'*).

Putting some warmth in my voice, I said, "Well! It's nice to see you, Gladys."

She straightened. "For a while there I thought you didn't remember me."

"Took me a moment," I admitted. "It's just that you're out of place. What brings you to Serenity?"

She nodded sagely. "I thought it would be best to move here."

"Ah," I said. "Is that right."

I smelled something, and it wasn't cookies. Nor was it perfume, because neither Gladys nor I was wearing any. Or if we were, not enough to overcome baked cookie.

Sensing my confusion, she said, "Because of, you know . . . the play?"

"Ah. The play."

78

A familiar scent now.

"So I got a job here in Serenity," she explained, "at the First National Bank — customer service teller." She shrugged. "It meant a cut in position and pay but will *definitely* be worth it. Just think, my first step on the way to Broadway!"

Mother. I smelled Mother.

I slid off the stool. "Why don't we go back to the kitchen and talk a bit." I raised my eyebrows. "I've got coffee and cookies."

"Sure!"

I led the way. Soon we were seated at the boomerang-top table across from each other with cups of java, the plate of what was left of the cookies serving as a centerpiece.

"Now, Gladys," I began. "What's all this about a play and Broadway?"

"Oh. Then your mother didn't tell you?"

"Not really."

She lowered her voice, keeping things confidential, even though we were alone. "Well, when the sheriff was working on those murders in Antiqua a few weeks ago, she came to see me at the bank and wanted some, er, *private* information about someone. When I told her that I couldn't share such things without a court order, she —"

"Promised you a part in *The Voice of the Turtle*."

79

That was the next production at the Playhouse, about to be cast.

Eyebrows in need of threading climbed the high forehead. "That's right!"

"Which part?" I asked, familiar with the script, as I was Mother's helper at the Playhouse (not by choice). "Sally Middleton or Olive Lashbrook?"

There was a male role that I felt it safe to eliminate.

"Olive," Gladys said, and smiled, then actually blushed.

Not the lead role, but easily the juicier part in the play — a sexpot, as they used to say in less enlightened times.

She was saying, "I've spent *weeks* memorizing *all* of my dialogue, so I am completely prepared, and ready to be the clay Mrs. Borne molds." She frowned. "The only thing is . . . I haven't heard a word from your mother. Even after I left her a phone message that I'd moved to town!"

"Is that right?"

Her words came in a rush now. "Then I saw the audition notice in the paper, which is for tomorrow night, and word at the bank is that she's in the hospital, and I got worried that she won't be able to keep her promise to me, and feared that perhaps I'd moved here for nothing."

Well, she could certainly handle a hunk of dialogue.

I leaned forward to give a comforting pat to the hand Gladys was resting on the table.

"Now, don't you fret. Mother is out of the hospital and will be at the audition. With bells on, as she puts it."

Not a bad idea — then I would know when she was coming.

I added, "And she always keeps her promises."

Most of the time.

Sometimes.

Okay, hardly ever.

Gladys gave a sigh of relief. "That's *so* good to hear."

Sensing a fragile psyche under there, I added, "And I just know you'll be wonderful in the part."

Memorable, at the very least.

She beamed. "Then *you* can see it too?"

"Uh — see what again?"

"My talent. Your mother told me it was palpable."

"Did she."

Gladys nodded. "She said she could tell just *talking* to me. Her exact words were, 'It oozes from every pore.' "

That sounded messy. "I, uh, am sure it does."

"Thank you!" She sipped the coffee.

I cocked my head. "So, then — you've had experience in theater? Local productions?"

She shook her head, and the mousy hair bounced. "Oh, no. Not even high school. I'm a diamond in the rough — which is another thing your mother said. But I'm not naive. Even a rough diamond needs polishing. And who better to polish me than an actress of your mother's skill, accomplishment, and charisma!"

Apparently Gladys hadn't seen Mother's performance in her musical version of *Everybody Loves Opal,* where, while mugging for the audience, she tumbled off the apron into the orchestra pit and got her foot stuck in the tuba. In a skillful, accomplished, charismatic way, of course.

But already I knew there was little if any hope of talking Gladys out of her folly. Mother deserved a good hiding for this, which was a prime example of the casual, unintended cruelty she could inflict.

"Do you know where the Serenity Playhouse is?" I asked. "Out in the country?"

She nodded. "I took a drive out there last night to have a look at the stage, but the doors were locked. There was a man there — at the other building? — but I didn't want to bother him." She leaned forward.

"Brandy? I won't have to *audition,* will I? I mean, because I was already promised the part."

"Shouldn't have to."

She sat back and let out a relieved sigh. "Good! Because I'd be much too nervous."

Oh boy.

Gently, I said, "Gladys . . . if you're too nervous for an audition, how are you going to feel performing in front of an audience? A packed house?"

"Oh, that's different!" she said. "I dealt with the public all the time, at the Antiqua bank. I gave reports at meetings too. And I have no trouble speaking in front of large groups — like the American Bankers Association convention last year in Atlanta, where my topic was customer service. There must have been a thousand people there for that! It's just . . . I'm really not comfortable competing."

"That *can* be unnerving," I said.

She looked at her watch. "I better get back to the bank. I said I'd only be gone a little while." She stood. "But I should go tomorrow night, anyway, right? Even though I already have the part?"

I felt bad for her, and I wished I could give you-know-who a kick in the seat of the pants about now.

I said, "Mother might want you to participate in the auditions of the other actors."

"You mean . . . read with them?"

"That's right. You know, do a scene or two
that you have with them. Make sure there's
good chemistry."

She beamed. Her smile did take the plain-
ness of her features to a pleasant place. "Oh,
I can do that. Will you tell Mrs. Borne I'll
be there?"

"You can count on that."

I walked with Gladys to the front door.

She asked, "Will I see you there?"

"Wouldn't miss it."

I had barely settled back onto the counter
stool when the door opened again, and an
unhappy-looking Tony strode in.

"Let me guess," I said. "You're upset with
Mother for ordering an autopsy on Mr. Sutter."

"You knew about that?" he asked, a hand
on the counter.

"She wanted me to go along with her, but
I've got a sensitive stomach." But not so
sensitive that I couldn't eat a half-dozen
cookies.

"But you *were* with her at the funeral
home."

I gulped. "Guilty as charged. But not

my idea!"

"I just got an earful from the stepson, who is rightly upset," he said. "This is exactly what I've been concerned about — Vivian overstepping her authority!"

Steam was practically coming out of his ears, and he usually held his temper in check around me. Sushi, who normally would be throwing herself at him by now, knew to stay put in her bed.

"I'm Mother's chauffeur," I reminded him, "not her keeper." I kept my tone nicely neutral.

He put hands on hips. "You're not even *trying* to stop her?"

That was enough. I got off the stool and came around the counter.

"No, I'm not," I said. "And do you know why?"

He blinked at me. "No. I really don't. You're almost always the steadying influence."

"Not this time around. I *want* her to go off the rails — I very much *want* her out there, acting so wacky that she'll get herself impeached."

He frowned, genuinely surprised by that. "And if people get hurt?"

I didn't have an answer for that, but fortunately his cell phone rang and he had to answer it.

"Cassato. . . . Yes, Tom. . . . Uh-huh . . ." A very long pause. "All right. Keep me in the loop."

He returned the cell to his pocket, his face more pink now than red.

"Apparently," Tony said, "the medical examiner feels the autopsy your mother demanded was" — he gestured with an open hand — "justified."

"Meaning?"

"Sutter's skull was cracked, and apparently not from a fall."

"Then Mother was *right* to order the procedure."

"But *wrong* in the way she went about it," he said. His sigh was an irritated rasp. "And now she'll be out there investigating, looking for suspects, muddying the waters."

"She *is* the sheriff."

"My patch, remember?"

"How's your blood pressure?"

He gave me a sour look.

I raised surrender palms. "Tony, I'm on your side — *our* side. I'll try to talk sense to Mother, and snitch on her when I can. But you may have to bring complaints against her with the county commissioner, who she's already in hot water with."

He said nothing for a moment. Then: "I'd

rather not do that. After all, she may be my future mother-in-law."

I smiled at that. Touched his arm. "Look, I happen to know Mother's going to be very busy with the play she's launching. Between that and her job, her snooping time will be limited. Her *own* patch will keep her plenty busy."

"Let's hope."

Awkwardly, we made a tentative plan to have dinner Saturday night at his cabin hideaway, and he left.

I returned to the computer and spent the next half an hour e-mailing auction houses and galleries to notify me if any new Tiffany lava vases came up for sale. And I made the same request with various eBay sellers, who wouldn't have as much scrutiny as auction houses or galleries, which would demand proof of ownership.

Since I hadn't had a single customer by four, I decided to close up early. I washed the dishes in the kitchen, brought in the flags, locked up, went out to the car with Sushi, and headed home.

In our own 1950s appointed kitchen, where the appliances were modern — albeit retro-looking (except for a vintage green Hamilton Beach malted milk mixer), I started to make supper . . . or dinner, if you're not a midwesterner . . . using a recipe Mother tore out from a magazine in her psychiatrist's waiting room, so I cannot credit the source.

She always steals the photo of the finished dish, too, so as to not, in her words, "risk a delicious recipe-less image causing further mental frustration among my doctor's other, far-more-troubled clients."

How thoughtful.

CHICKEN BREAST CASSEROLE

1 cup uncooked rice (brown or white)
1 (4-ounce) package of sliced, dried, or chipped beef
1 (10.5-ounce) can condensed (undiluted) mushroom soup
8 ounces sour cream
4 slices of bacon
4 chicken breasts, skinless

In the bottom of a buttered casserole dish, place the rice, then slices of chipped beef. Cover with the soup and then the sour cream. Wrap one piece of bacon around each chicken breast and place the breasts on top of the sour cream layer. Cover and cook at 250°F for 2 hours.

Serves 4

I was just popping the dish into the oven when I heard the front door open.

I left the kitchen and found Mother in the library/music/TV room, which made an olfactory cocktail out of musty old books, stinky ancient cornets (she used to play one), and the piney bouquet of air freshener.

Behind a turn-of-the-century-before-last stand-up piano, Mother stored an old-fashioned wooden chalkboard on wheels, which she was in the process of rolling out. The board was used to compile her suspect list on our cases.

From the open French doorway, I asked, "Shouldn't you wait for the pathologist's report?"

She looked at me. "It's never too early to get the little gray cells working."

I moved to the piano bench and sat. No stopping her, once she starts quoting Hercule Poirot.

Mother picked up a piece of white chalk from the lip of the board and wrote JAMES SUTTER SUSPECT LIST. Below that she put three headings: NAME, MOTIVE, OPPORTUNITY. She wrote GAVIN SUTTER, MONEY, and ? in the respective columns.

She stepped back and surveyed her work. "It's a start."

Over to you, Brandy, to throw the cold water on. "It's not your investigation, Mother."

"Whose is it, then?"

"Tony's. Stay out of it."

Not looking at me, she said, "I'll be discreet."

"When were you ever?"

Mother turned away from the board. "Dear, there wouldn't be an investigation if it weren't for me. A killer would have gotten off scot-free if I hadn't taken the initiative to call for an autopsy."

She wasn't wrong.

I said, "And I'm sure Tony is grateful. Now let him do his job."

Her eyes narrowed. "Are you friend or foe?"

"I'm a foe-for-your-own-good on this one."

Looking hurt (or pretending to be), she moaned, "Oh, 'how sharper than a serpent's tooth it is to have a thankless child!' "

She loved to trot out that Shakespearean nugget — I'd heard it a kazillion times. But it gave me the segue I needed.

"Speaking of plays," I said, "you'll never guess who dropped by the shop this afternoon."

"Who?"

90

"Gladys Gooch."

"Who?"

Doing her owl bit now, was she?

I said, "The bank manager from Antiqua?"

"Good Lord. Whatever did she want?"

"What do you think?"

Mother's face paled. It had all come back to her.

"Scoot over," she said, and joined me on the bench.

She stared into her fate. "I thought that overgrown waif would forget all about it. What does Gladys look like?"

My arms were folded, my smile smug. "The same."

"Then I'm ruined," she said.

"Not necessarily. In fact, a curvy woman in the part of Olive might be refreshing. That is, if she can act."

Mother's sigh came up from her toes. "No experience whatsoever."

"She's spoken in front of banking conferences."

"Oh, dear."

I sighed. "If only you'd promised her an audition, and not the part. *C'est la vie.*"

I was having too much fun at her expense, and almost felt a twinge of guilt. Emphasis on *almost.*

"Why don't you update the play?" I suggested. "Set it today instead of during World War II, and modernize the dated dialogue?"

Mother twisted toward me. "You may have something there." She sucked in air. "Perhaps turn it into a musical."

I frowned. "Where would you get the songs?"

"I'd write them myself."

"But you're opening in a month," I said. "Even Sondheim can't compose that fast."

Mother was positively giddy. "All I need are some new words! I'd use old standard tunes that are in public domain, like . . ." She thought a moment. " 'Beautiful Dreamer.' Just apply new lyrics to them." And she sang, " 'The voice of the turtle is calling to me. . . .' "

Ye gads!

"What if Gladys can't sing?" I asked.

Her smile was mildly crazed; it was early yet. "Then maybe she'll drop out. Anyway, I'll worry about that tomorrow night. When's supper? I want to get started on some lyrics. Possibly 'Danny Boy' — 'Oh Danny boy, the turtle, the turtle is callin' " . . . 'The Star-Spangled Banner,' perhaps — 'Oh, say can you hear, the voice of the turtle?' "

What had I unleashed?

VIVIAN'S TRASH 'N' TREASURES TIP
The higher the quality of the item, the
greater longevity the piece will have. I look
for antiques that will last at least another
twenty years, because that's how much time
I figure I have left.

Chapter Four:
In Which Vivian Can't Stand the Heat and Brandy Gets Out
of the Kitchen

After the chicken casserole supper, which was a little soupy because I took it out of the oven prematurely, Mother left the cleanup to me — which broke our rule of whoever cooks doesn't have to do the dishes.

But she had disappeared into the library, and began plunking away at the piano while singing another public domain ditty — "I'm Just Wild About Harry," changing Harry to William, the male lead in *The Voice of the Turtle.*

Which was more out of tune, the piano or Mother? Tough call.

Anyway, I had to get out of the house or lose what was left of my sanity, so I texted my BFF, Tina (short for Christina), to ask if I could hang out at her place for a few hours, immediately hearing back that she'd love to see me.

I abandoned the dirty dishes in the sink,

scrawled a note as to where I would be, and
— since Sushi was in with Mother and
seemed to be enjoying the caterwauling —
slipped out.

Tina; her husband, Kevin; and their two-
year-old daughter lived in a white ranch-
style house just outside of town on a bluff
overlooking the Mississippi River, a spectac-
ular year-round view. Nothing was more
relaxing to me than spending an hour or
two on the back patio with a glass of bubbly
— Tina always kept a bottle of champagne
on hand — chatting with my friend. We
would lazily watch the traffic on the water
— mostly speedboats, but also cargo-laden
barges, heading toward the lock and dam to
continue their travel downstream.

But right now dusk blanketed the bluff,
and a chilly fall wind was blowing, so I
doubted we'd be outside, even with the gas
fire pit going.

A year younger than me, Tina had become
my fast friend in high school, when yours
truly came around a hall corner after school
and found some senior girls picking on her.
I'd let them know how I felt about bullying
in the kind of no uncertain terms that would
make the most seasoned sailor blush. Later,
Tina and I both attended Serenity Community College, and — after we'd finished

our two-year stint — I'd put a crimp in our friendship by marrying Roger, a broker in Chicago I'd met, who was ten years my senior.

While I truly did love Roger, I had another agenda, too, which was to get away from Mother. Our union produced a wonderful son, Jake (now fourteen), who has lived with his father since the divorce but comes to stay with Mother and me during school breaks. Jake has been known to get caught up (along with me) in Mother's investigative shenanigans, enjoying the experience more than I do.

I won't go into how I busted up my marriage by way of a poor decision at a Serenity High class reunion, fueled by how miscast I'd been as the wife of a big-time financial broker. Let's leave it at this: Roger has since made peace with me, and I with him, and he's now married to a strong, smart woman who is just the kind of partner he needed.

As for Tina, she married Kevin, a terrific guy who worked for a pharmaceutical company, and they stayed in Serenity, intending to start a family, but then life threw them a curve. Tina got breast cancer and, while aggressive treatments gave her the highest chance, they also made Tina infertile. So I'd offered to be their surrogate, using Tina's eggs harvested before the treatments began. Nine months later came an adorable little baby girl they named Brandy.

The porch light was on, and Tina answered the bell, looking as beautiful as ever — trim but shapely in a black cashmere sweater and skinny jeans, her lovely features framed by natural blond hair that fell to her shoulders like liquid gold, her wide smile revealing perfect teeth. I know, I should hate her.

"Hey, stranger," she said.

I smiled back at her, if less perfectly. "Sorry it's been so long."

"Well, you're here now. That's what counts."

"And you're here for me when I need safe harbor from Mother, and that *really* counts."

I stepped inside, and she took my hand.

Immediately I was accosted by a tiny cherub attired in pink, with a crown of yellow curls, brown eyes, and a button nose. She was clutching a book half her size.

"Be-be, read me," she squeaked to me, not quite yet able to pronounce "Brandy."

I scooped my little namesake up and held her close, taking in the scent of her hair and her baby-powdered skin, feeling the smoothness of her cheek against mine.

Have to be frank with you. Being around the toddler was both joyous and painful for me. You see, I was not only her surrogate mother, I was her natural mother, too. When all Tina's harvested eggs had been tried, with no results, the doctors took some of mine.

Kevin materialized in T-shirt and jeans, a hunk of a guy with sandy-blond hair and a handsome, almost too-good-to-be-true face.

"Brandy," he announced. "You need a bath."

"Me or her?" I asked.

"I'll let that one pass," he said with a smirk, and reached for Be-Be, who put up a fuss until I promised to read to her afterward.

Then Kevin hoisted his daughter up onto his shoulders and hauled the giggling girl off to the bathroom.

Tina, watching from the sidelines, smiled and said, "That will take a while, so we'll have plenty of time to talk. Be-Be loves a bath, once she gets in there with all her toys, and Mr. Bubble does his magic."

"Mr. Bubble! They still make that stuff?"

"Oh, yes. Kevin likes it too."

"A luxury I never enjoyed."

Mother had used dishwashing detergent to make bubbles for me, as if I were a dirty pan. Of course, sometimes in childhood I *did* have a dirty pan. No wonder my skin always itched.

My friend curled a finger. "Come with me. You can pour your heart out while I pour champagne. I take it that's the main reason for the visit."

"You know me too well."

In the modern kitchen, I sat in the dining area at the round un-modern oak table while Tina rummaged in the fridge, then brought over a bottle of bubbly. We preferred the cheap stuff — expensive champagne gave us both stomachaches.

Returning to a cupboard for two flute glasses, she quipped, "Bette Davis once said, 'There comes a time in every woman's life when the only thing that helps is a glass of champagne.' "

"Only lately," I said, "there are *lots* of times in my life when that kind of help is needed."

Standing at the table, Tina popped the cork, then poured the sparkling beige liquid into both glasses and handed me a brimming flute glass. I took a sip, the bubbles tickling my nose. Bette Davis was right; I immediately felt better.

"Unload," she said, sliding into the chair next to me.

I did, beginning with my continued servitude as Mother's chauffeur, her modus operandi of overstepping her authority as sheriff, the strain on my relationship with Tony, and finally the inattention given to our antiques shop, which (should it continue) could put us out of business.

"Wow," Tina said. "You do have a lot on your shoulders. Have you talked with your therapist?"

"Not lately."

"Why?"

"You're a lot cheaper. Plus, champagne."

She smiled. "Glad to provide gratis therapy, as long as you're satisfied with the cheap bubbly prescription."

"What is your therapeutic guidance, Doctor?"

"Stay on the Prozac."

"That's what my therapist always says."

Tina cocked her head. "Is there anything else bothering you? Not that all of that isn't plenty."

"Saved the best for last."

"Let's have it."

"It's pretty heavy."

"I can take it, Brandy. Shoot."

I threw up my hands. "The fall fashions suck! Where are the cute clothes?"

"I *know*!" she said. "I don't see anything

in the stores or online that's better than what I already have."

We trashed the fashion industry for a while, then Tina said, "I think we're about due for a road trip, don't you?"

"Absotively," I said, and clinked my glass with hers.

Tina and I were serious veterans of the shopping wars, sustaining battle scars — me, a black eye; Tina, a sprained finger — during hand-to-hand combat with the enemy (fellow shoppers). Our skills had been honed over the years, enabling us to avoid enemy lines (by using the checkout in the men's department), target the sales (usually in the back of the store), and uncover other combatant's subterfuge (hiding items in a different section for later retrieval). Once, Tina and I infiltrated nine shopping centers in the greater Chicago area in a single day! Now that was a decisive victory making D-Day pale in comparison.

We discussed our road trip strategy for a while, and then Kevin appeared, saying, "Teen, she wants you to read first, then Brandy."

Tina smiled. "That way she can prolong bedtime. Take my place, Kev?"

"Glad to."

She departed, and Kevin got a beer from

the fridge, then joined me.

"How's the new job?" I asked.

Kevin had left the pharmaceutical business, which required him to travel more than he liked, in favor of becoming an independent insurance agent, using many different carriers instead of just one, like State Farm, for instance.

"Job's going well," Kevin said. "I'm mostly dealing with health insurance, which can be a real challenge nowadays. But in another year or two, I'll be able to buy into a partnership."

"With Cliff Reed?"

Kevin nodded. "He handles home and auto and business coverage right now. But I'll be taking over some of that, because he's going to be extra busy for a while."

"Oh?"

He took a gulp from the can. "Cliff is knee-deep, dealing with the policies of both James Sutter and Benjamin Wentworth."

Now I nodded. "Coverage for the mansion, and the antiques. Big losses on both."

Another swig of beer. "Yeah, what a mess! Not so much the mansion, which is pretty straightforward . . . although the cause of the fire has to be determined before there's a payout."

"In case it was arson."

"Right."

I leaned forward. "You don't think James Sutter himself might have started it, do you? And couldn't make it out of there in time?"

He didn't speak for a moment, then added cryptically, "All I can say is, there are people who are glad that the mansion is gone."

I didn't press him. This was really none of my business, although I could almost hear Mother's voice in my ear, egging me on.

But without prompting, Kevin continued. "The real headache is with the antiques."

"Oh? How much coverage are we talking?"

"A million."

I whistled. "The carrier holding that policy is *not* going to be thrilled."

Kevin shrugged. "Naturally, they'll look for ways to avoid paying up. And even if they express a willingness to do so, it could take *years*, verifying all the antiques. They'll stretch it out, hoping for a lesser settlement."

"That's why our merchandise at the shop isn't covered," I said, with a humorless half smile. "Too much trouble."

"Your situation is different, Brandy. You can easily get business coverage without costly appraisals, by listing and keeping track of your inventory. Things you're already doing."

"I guess didn't realize that. I'll talk to Mother."

"You really should."

Tina popped into the kitchen. "The con is yours, Captain," she told me.

I left the table to read to Be-Be. Or I should say, for her to read to me, mostly, since she had the book completely memorized.

The following morning, Wednesday, I took Sushi and drove Mother in the C-Max to her office at the county jail, dropped her off, then parked a few blocks away in the lot of the First National Bank, where Cliff Reed had his office on the building's top floor.

The night before, after tucking myself into bed, I'd realized that something I owned, something very precious to me, was not insured: my rare 1930s bird's-eye maple Art Deco bedroom set: head- and footboard, six-drawer dresser, pair of nightstands, plus a pedestal vanity with huge half-circle mirror spanning its length.

Meaning to be gone just a few minutes, I left Sushi in the car, went into the bank, and took the elevator to the third floor. In the office I approached the receptionist — a young woman with strawberry blond hair and noticeable curves — and introduced myself. I was about to ask for an appointment with Cliff when the agent himself appeared.

"Brandy, right?" he asked, with a mild smile. "I spotted you from the hall."

In his late forties or perhaps early fifties, Cliff Reed had light brown hair, a matching mustache, and an open face one could readily trust. He was wearing a white shirt with sleeves rolled back, paisley-patterned silk tie, dark gray dress slacks, and — for a touch of rebellion — Nikes.

"Yes, hi. And you're Cliff."

"I'm Cliff. Are you wanting to see Kevin or me?"

"You. I already have health insurance."

The agent checked his watch, glanced up with the smile again. "I have a little time before my next appointment. Care to fill it?"

"I'd be grateful," I said. "Save me another trip."

I followed him down a carpeted hallway past a closed door with Kevin's name, the murmur of voices indicating Tina's hubby was with a client. Cliff's office was at the end of the hallway, and I stepped into a spacious, nicely appointed room with a long window giving a picturesque view of the river.

To the right was a round conference table and four chairs, to the left a wine-colored leather couch and glass coffee table, and straight ahead, in front of the windows, a mahogany desk with a brown leather swivel chair. The place whispered money, but at least it didn't shout.

A wide windowsill displayed a variety of family photos, showcasing Cliff's wife and two sons at various stages of their lives. Viewing the pictures from left to right, I saw the two young sons grow up, graduate from high school, then college, and get married. The few photos that included Cliff revealed he'd put on some weight, lost some hair, and developed the appropriate lines on his face for a man with a family and a business to look after.

On the other hand, his attractive brunette wife didn't look any different from photo to photo; in fact, after the boys had started their own families, she appeared to have grown younger. The effects of healthy living? Or the skill of a surgeon's hand?

Cliff moved to his chair, where his suit jacket hung on the back, and I selected one of two client chairs in front of the cluttered desk.

When we'd both settled, he asked, "How is your mother doing?"

"Fine. Back at work."

"Good to hear. That's a big job for someone to tackle without much experience . . . meaning no offense."

"Couldn't agree more."

He chuckled. "I don't know Vivian well, but I understand she can be somewhat . . . headstrong?"

"I *do* know her well, and that's an understatement."

The mild smile just went on forever. "What can I do for you, Brandy?"

"I have an antique bedroom set. Or at least a collectible one. Art Deco, dates to the thirties."

I handed him my phone with the pictures I'd taken, and he scrolled through them.

"Lovely," he said, returning the photos. "I agree these pieces should be insured. Do you have another home insurance agent?"

"No, but Mother does."

He shrugged. "In that case, the easiest thing for you to do is add the coverage for the bedroom set to her existing policy."

"I'd rather not do that."

Flipped a hand. "It would be cheaper than having a separate one with me."

I shook my head. "I'd like my own policy,

in my own name."

I didn't want to tell him that on several occasions, when Mother went off her meds, financial concerns had gone by the wayside, including the lapsing of several insurance policies.

So I said, "That way I'll know for sure that it's covered."

"Makes sense," Cliff said. "I work with several companies that specialize in coverage for antiques and collectibles."

"Maybe not the one you used to insure the Wentworth antiques," I quipped, then immediately regretted it.

He seemed to study me. "Where did you hear that?"

Uh-oh. I didn't want to mention Kevin, so I laid the blame on a dead man.

"James Sutter," I said, and explained how, on the afternoon before the fire, Sutter had talked about having separate insurance policies on the mansion and its antiques.

"Anyway," I rambled on, "I was kidding on the square, figuring that company's premiums might go up, after the dust settles."

Cliff sat forward. "You say you were there the afternoon before the fire?"

"Yes. Mother and I were."

The agent grew keenly interested. "Did

Mr. Sutter show you around?"

I gave him a tiny shrug. "Just the first floor. The second was being painted and plastered."

Cliff nodded, then said, "You know, this could be very useful to the insurance investigation."

"Regarding?"

"What you and Vivian saw."

"The antiques, you mean."

His eyebrows rose. "It would help establish what was there."

Why? Was there some doubt?

Cliff continued, "I'd appreciate it if you were willing to meet with the investigator."

"All right." Another little shrug. "But Mother would be a better bet, since she's the one familiar with the contents of the mansion. She toured the place more than once."

And if Mother wanted to mention the absence of the Tiffany vase, that was up to her.

I gave Cliff our contact information.

Moving on to the reason for my visit, the agent proceeded to give me some homework — a general form to fill out regarding the original purchase price of the bedroom set, from whom and when, and instructions on obtaining a qualified appraisal. I would need to provide physical photos of each piece of furniture. Then, after I return the form, he'll submit it to several insurance companies, who will come back with quotes, which he'll compare for the best price.

I thanked Cliff for working me into his busy schedule, took my homework assignment, and left. On my way out, I'd intended to say hello to Kevin, but his door was still closed, so I moved on.

Then I spotted Gavin Sutter in the reception area, rising from a chair in response to the receptionist's "Cliff will see you now," and I froze.

Chagrined by the scene Mother had created at the Dunn funeral home, I backtracked; spotted a bathroom; and, being a chicken at heart, ducked inside to avoid passing Gavin in the hallway.

The bathroom must have shared a wall with Cliff's office, because I heard the agent's muffled greeting, followed by the sound of his office door closing.

I was about to leave when a vocal exchange between the men reached my ears.

"What the hell *happened,* Cliff?"

"How the fudge should *I* know!"

Okay, Cliff didn't say *fudge.*

At that point, the voices lowered, and I couldn't make out what was said anymore, even with my ear to the wall.

The locked bathroom doorknob jiggled, and I flushed, ran some sink water, and departed, giving the waiting female a smile and "Too much coffee," to which she replied, "Me too."

I made my way to the reception area, where the strawberry blonde was engaged on the phone, and I headed toward the front door just as it opened.

A white-haired, nicely tanned distinguished-looking gentleman entered. He wore a beige Burberry trench coat, open to reveal a tailored navy suit, gray shirt, and silver tie. If I'd been in Beverly Hills, I might have thought he was a retired movie star.

He held the door for me, I thanked him, and as I went on through, I heard the receptionist say, "Good morning, Mr. Wentworth. Mr. Sutter is already here. You can go on back."

Hmmm. Why would Cliff meet with Sutter and Wentworth at the same time? Granted, Cliff was the agent for both men, each wanting his policy payout; but the timing seemed a little odd. Still, the mansion and furnishings *were* intertwined.

I returned to my car, where Sushi, indignant at having been ditched for so long, would not look at me. She had a snaggletooth, anyway, but with her jaw jutting out the way it now did, she looked even more comical.

"Sorry," I said, and proceeded to explain what had kept me, as if she could understand. And can you swear she didn't?

At a few minutes before ten, we arrived at our shop, and after dutifully hoisting the appropriate flags, I was about to make coffee and cookies but never got a chance.

Antiques merchants will tell you that there are predictable patterns to the flow of customer traffic. For instance, Saturdays are busy after payday (mornings more than afternoons), as are sunny days (all seasons) and Christmastime (folks looking for something unique, or wanting to recapture childhood holiday memories). But this was not Saturday, or sunny, or Christmas.

So go figure.

I was kept hopping for two straight hours by people who actually bought things, bringing in an influx of much-needed cash. And I had to give Mother the credit for the sales. Since she'd become busy as sheriff, we've been supplying the shop with the stash of stuff she'd collected over the years (mostly acquired when she was off her meds), which had consumed our one-car garage.

Among the items unloaded were a Barbie Disco portable record player with microphone (BYOBG — Bring Your Own Bee Gees record); a 1940s department store lady's head and décolleté (Ginger Rogers look-alike) used to display necklaces and that I wanted for myself (Mother said fine, if I paid for it); a battered leather case of old dental tools (I didn't ask the man what he planned on doing with it); and a vintage roll of children's wallpaper featuring Howdy Doody, Clarabelle, Mr. Bluster, and Mother's favorite character from the old TV kiddie show (Flub-A-Dub, which prompted her, for reasons unknown, to sing, "Ta-ra-ra Boom-de-ay!").

By around noon, the locusts had thinned and I'd raked in over five hundred smackers. Maybe Mother should go off her meds more often. That was when Mother blew in and showed me the error of my thinking.

Her face was flushed, eyes wilder than usual behind the large lenses.

I braced myself, glad to have the counter between us.

"Guess what!" she exclaimed.

I gave it a shot. "Your Vespa arrived."

"No! Wait, has it?"

"How should I know?"

She rushed around the counter like a thief

with a gun. "If you're going to be capricious, I won't tell you."

"Fine with that." My eyes returned to the computer screen.

She stood there. "I just thought you'd be interested."

"Any special reason?"

Excitement returned to her face. "I got a copy of Tom Peak's autopsy report."

That got my attention, all right.

I blurted, *"How?"* I figured, after throwing her out of the procedure, the medical examiner would be keeping that report under lock and key.

"What you don't know," she replied somewhat huffily, "won't hurt you. Or me. Or anyone!"

But what I *did* know was that — like Gladys Gooch — some poor soul had surely been promised something.

Mother was saying, "Preliminary testing of the esophagus and lungs show no signs of smoke inhalation."

Now she had me. Really had me.

I said, "Then Mr. Sutter was dead *before* the fire started!"

She was nodding, her smile very proud of itself. "That was Tom's conclusion, confirmed by the coroner. Of course, results from more extensive testing of the tissue have yet to come back, but that could take months. In the meantime, the death will be treated as a homicide." She paused. "And that's why I need *your* help."

I gave her a hard stare. "You want me to wheedle information out of Tony."

She feigned surprise, one hand going to her chest. "Why, dear, I'd *never* ask that of you! Now that you lovebirds are back on an even keel, I wouldn't *dream* of rocking the boat."

Was that two mixed metaphors, or three?

"But," she continued, "should the chief *happen* to let something slip about the investigation during pillow talk . . . you *will* tell your dear old mother, won't you?"

"Tony won't let something slip," I said, "on or off the pillow. And if he did, I wouldn't betray him."

Her chin came up. "How *can* you be so cruel?"

"I had a good teacher. But, listen . . . if you stay out of Tony's way on this, I will share something I found out."

She brightened. "What's that, dear?"

"Cliff Reed, the insurance agent, is handling the claims for both Gavin Sutter and Benjamin Wentworth."

"Oh, I already know that."

"Okay. But did you know *this*. . . ."

And I told Mother where I'd gone after dropping her off at the jail, and what I'd heard and seen there.

After which she said, "While I agree it's unusual for Cliff to meet jointly with two different clients, it's the exchange between Gavin and Cliff before Benjamin arrived that interests me. I wish you'd been privy to more in the privy." She paused, smiling at her own cleverness; then, dead serious, she asked, "What was your initial impression?"

I thought back. "I guess that . . . something they were involved in together went wrong."

"Which might possibly include Mr. Wentworth."

"Possibly." Time to change the subject. "Are you ready for the auditions this evening?"

"I'm never *not* ready," she sniffed. "And I plan to share with the gang a song I've just penned."

" 'I'm Just Wild About William'?"

"That needed more work. I mean, really, he's 'Bill' in the play, not William, and 'Bill' doesn't scan well. No, I've worked up what will be the play's signature song, set to 'The Bells of St. Mary's.' I think Bing would be pleased." She began to warble, *"The voice of the turtle is calling to me —"*

116

I put a hand out to stop her. "I think I'd like to be surprised tonight, like everyone else."

"As you wish."

"You *know* you'll have to cast her."

"Who, dear?"

"Don't play dumb — that's your least convincing role. You have to cast *Gladys*. Otherwise, word will get around that Vivian Borne doesn't keep her promises, and you'll never again get anyone else to snitch — for example, whomever you wheedled that autopsy report out of."

She was frowning, but she said, "Good point. I'm hoping Gladys will have a change of mind, once she gets onstage, and realizes she's out of her depth."

I shook my head. "I've talked with her. She'd rather sink the ship and take everyone down with her."

Mother sighed. "Then I'd best bring all of my directing skills to bear, else face embarrassment."

"More like ruin. You've weathered embarrassment plenty of times."

A customer came in, ending our conversation, and Mother slipped away, sheriff duty calling.

The rest of the afternoon was slow — all lookers and no takers — and I was relieved when five o'clock crawled around.

I was about to shut down the computer when an alert came onto the screen.

A Tiffany vase had just been posted for sale on the website of an antique shop in Chicago. Price upon request.

The item, as pictured, was awfully familiar.

It seemed to be the Wentworth vase, all right.

A TRASH 'N' TREASURES TIP

When buying online, it's important to add to the purchase price the cost of shipping. More than once I thought I snagged a bargain, only to have the postage and handling run more than the item itself.

CHAPTER FIVE:
IN WHICH THE BALL LANDS IN VIVIAN'S COURT AND BRANDY GOES OUT OF BOUNDS

I decided to postpone telling Mother about the appearance of the Tiffany vase online, knowing she would have enough on her mind with the auditions this evening. And, anyway, I preferred to keep her focus on theater and not homicide. The latter was Tony's bailiwick, after all — within the city limits, anyway.

The Playhouse Theater, situated among cornfields about ten miles west of town, began as an old barn where community actors would gather and perform on a makeshift stage to the delight of family and friends. In those days, you must have been able to imagine Judy Garland and Mickey Rooney yelling, "Come on, gang — let's put on a show and save the farm!"

Over the years, however, the barn had been transformed into a modern theatrical facility — thanks to Mother's relentless haranguing for donations from Serenity's wealthiest residents, who were often up for supporting the local arts (and getting Vivian Borne off their backs) — with new additions, periodic remodeling, and a state-of-the-art auditorium. About the only thing left of the original structure was its rooster weather vane.

And Mother's participation onstage had also been a big part of this transformation, as any play Vivian Borne appeared in, or even just directed, always drew eager crowds who knew anything could happen. And often did.

Like the aforementioned *Everybody Loves Opal* foot-in-the-tuba debacle, or when her production of *My Fair Lady* included several real horses running across the stage in the Ascot scene, causing a panic in the auditorium, not to mention some messy cleanup. And, my favorite, Mother's insistence on using real fireworks in *You Can't Take It with You,* which set the curtains ablaze and nearly burned down the theater. But beautiful new fire retardant curtains did result, thanks to those benefactors.

About half an hour before the six o'clock call, Mother (in her favorite emerald green velour pants suit) and I (in a long gray sweater and black leggings) pulled in in our C-Max, the parking lot otherwise empty.

Sushi was with us because she loved to run all around inside the facility, and somehow could sense when the theater was our destination. Perhaps this was due to key words in our conversation, or possibly Mother lugging her tote bag of scripts and such. At any rate, I'd made bringing Soosh along to the theater a permanent practice, ever since once I'd left her home and she vindictively chewed up my new Jimmy Choos.

Two cars were parked around back near the stage door entrance — the black Mazda belonging to stage manager Miguel, and Gladys Gooch's blue Toyota. How did I identify the latter vehicle as Ms. Gooch's? The former-bank-manager-turned-teller was standing next to it.

As soon as we exited our vehicle, with me carrying Sushi and Mother her tote bag, Gladys came at us like an eager, perhaps mildly rabid puppy. Even Sushi was taken aback.

"I am *so* excited," she exclaimed.

"Lovely to see you, dear," Mother said, her performance of the line mediocre at best.

Mother gave her prospective casting choice the eye, in particular the woman's bland navy suit and prim white blouse.

She said to Gladys, "You *are* aware you're playing a promiscuous temptress."

"Well . . . I . . . just came from the bank. That kind of look is not encouraged there."

"Ah, understood," Mother said, backpedaling.

"You look fine, Gladys," I said, having already flashed Mother a reproving glance. "Most of the actors will have come straight from work. Anyway, costumes aren't usually a part of Playhouse auditions."

"I could unbutton my blouse a little," the woman suggested uneasily.

"That won't be necessary, dear," Mother said, borderline obsequious now. "I'll merely be introducing you tonight. We need not call upon your talents."

Unbuttoned or otherwise.

Disappointment clouded the plump face. "I won't be reading lines with the others?"

"Not until I've had a chance to see you in action," Mother replied. "And we've had a chance to work together a bit."

Probably a wise decision.

Mother went on, "So you'll just be observing. Getting a feel for the Playhouse. Sizing up your fellow thespians."

"Oh. Thespian is an actor, right?"

"It is indeed, dear. For now, just take a seat out front until I introduce you."

"Okay. Anywhere in particular?"

"Somewhere toward the back. It will give you a panoramic effect. The full . . ."

Mother searched for the word.

"Monty?" I suggested.

She frowned at me. "The full Playhouse experience."

Of people not in costume, on a bare-bones suggestion of a set, reading from scripts. Yup, everything but the chandelier falling in *Phantom of the Opera*.

Gladys hesitated, as if expecting us all to go inside the building together, but Mother stood her ground, saying, "Best you go on in the front way, dear. I don't want to be seen as playing favorites."

Gladys nodded, turned, and walked away.

When Mother's acting discovery had disappeared around the building, we remained paused at the stage door.

Mother said, "Brandy, darling, I'm afraid this may well bring down the curtain on my directing days at the Playhouse."

"Gladys may work out." Or a year from now the Playhouse might just be a barn again.

Wearing a wicked smile, Mother said, "But I *do* have one ace up my sleeve."

"What would that be?"

"Fire the girl opening night, gently of

course, and play Olive myself."

"A seventy-something sexpot."

Her eyes flared behind the big lenses. "Well, that remark is both sexist *and* ageist!"

"You're right," I admitted. This *would* be her last Playhouse play.

Sushi, impatient to go inside, barked.

The stage door opened into a long corridor leading to the shop and maintenance room at left and dressing, wardrobe, and prop rooms at right.

We hadn't taken but a few steps before Miguel — wearing his signature black T-shirt and jeans — entered the hallway, coming from the back of the stage.

"We're going to be shorthanded," he said with a frown. "Leon didn't show up when he was scheduled, and he doesn't answer his cell."

Leon, the janitor, often helped out during auditions. Mother had gone out on a limb hiring the middle-aged man, despite his having a criminal record. By all accounts, Leon was now trustworthy, cordial, good at his job, and willing to do tasks outside his province.

"Knowing our janitor," Mother said, "he must have been taken ill."

"Which," the stage manager groused,

"doesn't do us any good at the moment."

Miguel had more to say, but I didn't hear it. Because as soon as he announced they were going to be shorthanded, I began fading back with Sushi, slinking down the corridor to duck into the first door I could, which was one of the principal's dressing rooms.

Nonetheless I could hear Mother boom, "Now *where* did that girl go?"

So I waited a full minute before sticking my head out.

"Close call," I whispered to Sushi.

Mother had often roped me into helping at the Playhouse, and while most of the time I put up with it, this evening I wanted to watch from the audience. I was truly curious to see how Mother would handle an open audition in which she had already cast a key role, and done so with a nonveteran player at the Playhouse.

"What say we hide out in the prop room for a while?" I asked Sushi.

As soon as I'd said the words *prop room,* Sushi's tail began to switch back and forth, because she loved that area as much as I did.

And why not? Where else could you find a shrunken head, a Roman helmet, fake snowballs, a gorilla suit, and a gun that fired flowers, all conveniently assembled in one place? And where else in a busy theater, bustling with the needs of a soon-to-be-production, could you hide away and take a nap?

Not that I was planning on a nap. I'd just stay in there long enough for technical problems to get solved. Then, after the actors arrived, Sushi and I would go sit in the dark in the back row of the theater. Maybe we'd keep Gladys company.

In the prop room, I played with a small hand-control-operated Audrey II from *Little Shop of Horrors,* while Sushi attacked the large black toy dog with horns and glowing eyes from Mother's all-female-cast version of *The Hound of the Baskervilles.* (She had played Sheryl Holmes.)

About ten minutes after six, I scooped Sushi up and departed the prop room, using an exit into the lobby that allowed me to slip into the theater through the main auditorium doors.

We settled in the back center row, as planned.

The stage was empty but for a couch and two chairs, to accommodate a scene between the characters of Sally and Bill, as selected by Mother for the tryouts.

She was down in front of the orchestra

pit, facing a group of hopefuls who had spread themselves out in the first several rows. The group was on the smallish side for an audition — about a dozen local actors — because of the small cast of only three characters. Well, two characters now, but they didn't know that yet.

Mother addressed them, coming in and out of her pretentious British accent. "Thank you one and all for coming out to the thee-ah-tah this evening. This is going to be a groundbreaking production of *Voice,* because of some innovative changes I am implementing . . ."

Miguel was standing off to her right, and even from the back row, I could see his body stiffen, indicating all of this "innovation" was news to him.

". . . but first," the grand dame went on, "I must make an announcement regarding the role of Olive, which, no doubt, will disappoint those of you hoping to audition for the part." She paused, then said, bringing gravitas to her words, "It has been filled."

Mother's natural bent toward the overdramatic made the situation worse than it already was. This brought unhappy responses from some of the women, and the stage manager moved closer to Mother, with

127

an expression that was nearly a scowl.

"Why was I not informed?" he demanded.

"I'm informing you now, dear," Mother replied.

"And just *who* has the part?" he asked.

"Miss Gladys Gooch," she said, her eyes searching the auditorium seats, as she called out. "Gladys, please stand, darling."

I hadn't noticed her, well off to my right. As the potential sexpot got to her feet, heads craned for a look.

"And what else exactly has she done?" Miguel asked Mother.

Very bad form for Miguel, who should not have been confronting the director that way, even if she deserved it. Which, of course, she did.

"Why, what *hasn't* she done!" Mother responded rhetorically. "Miss Gooch just moved here from Wisconsin and is a recent graduate of the Theater of Performing Arts of . . ." And here Mother paused, because she had great difficulty not giving a Jerry Lewis spin to the following word. "Sheboygan."

And completely failed. She might as well have added, *"Laaaaaddeeee!"*

Recovering, she waved a dismissive hand at a slightly bewildered Gladys. "Thank you, dear, you may be seated."

She did.

Miguel grumbled something I couldn't make out.

Mother, ignoring him, said, "Those of you here to audition for the part of Olive are welcome to do so for the *leading* role of Sally."

This did not appease several actresses, who got irritatedly to their feet and headed to the exit door, stage right. One snapped, "What's the point? It's gonna be Kimberly, anyway."

Kimberly Summers, seated front row center, was a pretty blonde in her mid-twenties who had recently advanced from ingenue parts to leads and was a favorite of Serenity audiences. My money was on her, as well.

Mother, anxious to move on, cleared her throat to get the actors' attention back where it belonged: herself. "What will make this production unique is that it will *not* be set during World War Two, rather present day. Therefore, the character of Bill is on leave from Iraq or Afghanistan, which will mean changing some of the dialogue. For example, in act one, scene two, Bill talks about his time spent in Paris —"

"You can't *do* that!" Miguel said.

Mother arched an eyebrow. "Do what, dear?"

"Rewrite the dialogue!"

Mother faced him. "I certainly can. I'm also mounting it as a musical version, introducing a few songs, which I've already written."

"You can't do *that,* either! Not without the playwright's permission."

"Well, I'm certainly aware of that," she huffed. "But contacting the playwright would be rather difficult, considering that John Van Druten is long gone. Perhaps you have a Ouija board handy?"

"That he's no longer living does not matter," Miguel said tersely. "You *still* have to contact the play's publisher, who will notify Van Druten's estate for their approval." He paused. "All that will take time, and I doubt it will be allowed, in any case."

Mother, hands on hips, lifted her chin regally. "It's a moot point, my dear Miguel. We're talking about a three-week-run that will be over with by the time any publisher or the estate hears about it and demands a cease and desist. Besides, I'm doing them a service. Generating new interest in a severely out-of-date property."

Miguel guffawed, then said flatly, "*You* are doing John Van Druten a service? The man who also wrote *Bell, Book and Candle*?"

"Not him, dear," Mother replied, "the estate. Were you aware that for the first time in six decades *The Voice of the Turtle* has failed to make the top ten list of community theater productions? *That* translates into lost revenue for the late playwright's heirs."

Her words seemed to be lost on Miguel, who pointed a scolding finger. "If you go ahead with this, Vivian, then *you* will take full responsibility for any repercussions."

"Agreed," Mother said, nonplused.

"Fine," the stage manager said. "And I intend to go on record with the Playhouse board."

A male in the audience waved a hand. "Mrs. Borne, will Bill have to sing?"

"Yes, he will."

"But, uh . . . singing wasn't indicated as a requirement. And it's just not part of my skill set."

Mother shrugged one shoulder. "Neither could Rex Harrison in *My Fair Lady,* but he won the Academy Award for Best Actor." She clapped her hands twice. "Now, any other questions before we begin?"

Sushi squirmed in a way that told me she had urgent needs. Which was my fault, because I hadn't properly given her time to tend to business before we'd left home,

Mother being in such a hurry.

I retraced my steps into the lobby, through the door leading to props, wardrobe, and the dressing rooms, then out the stage door.

The night was chilly, and I'd left my coat in the car, but figured Sushi wouldn't keep me out too long . . . but I was wrong. After she'd trotted to a patch of grass and squatted, she scampered off toward the storage building. Calling her to come back would be futile, so I ran after her.

The windowless building, bathed in a security light, had a front entrance door and, on the side, a double-size garage door, which was where Sushi was heading for some unknown reason.

Before I could reach her, the little rascal flattened herself and crawled under the garage door, which hadn't been closed completely.

I went to the front entrance, found it locked, and returned to the partially raised door.

Down on my hands and knees, I yelled into the void. "Sushi! Come here!"

No doggie. I hollered again. Still no Sushi. In anger, I pushed upward on the garage door, and it opened high enough for me to crawl under.

Inside I fumbled in the dark for a wall

switch, found one, and flicked several lights on. Then I stood, amazed at the amount of stuff that had been amassed over the years. Even Mother's trash-and-treasures garage at home was no competition.

Furniture pieces were stacked on top of each other, chunks of dismantled sets leaned against walls, and fake potted ferns and small trees made a forest in which lurked big props like the grown Audrey II and a full-size Santa's sleigh. The prop room paled in comparison. No wonder Sushi wanted inside.

Pathways took me here and there, sometimes leading to dead ends, and all the while I kept calling to her.

Frustration was turning to worry when something touched my shoulder, and I yelped.

"What are you doing in here?" Miguel asked gruffly.

I had to wait a moment until my heart stopped pounding. "Trying to find Sushi."

"What made you think she's in here?"

I told him that the garage door had been partially open and she went in under it. And I had pulled the door up enough to squeeze under myself.

"You better find her," the stage manager said. "Since the weather turned cool, Leon's put poison out for the rats that have come in from the cornfields."

While I didn't think Sushi's rarefied palate would include eating poison, Miguel's words nonetheless did cause alarm. So I resorted to a ruse with Sushi that I used only sparingly, for fear it would one day no longer work.

"Cookie, cookie, cookie," I called out.

She might have been prowling nearby — I'm not really sure — but suddenly the doggie was at my feet.

Both relieved and mad, I scooped her up, and when she saw I had no cookie, her little jaw jutted out accusingly. I'd have to make sure all my shoes were up and off the floor at home.

I thanked Miguel for his warning.

"Lucky I was out for a smoke," he said, "and saw the light on in the building."

An awkward silence.

"How are the auditions going?" I asked.

He grunted. "They're over already. Most everyone left after Vivian announced it was a musical." He paused. "But Kimberly and Zefross stayed, and got the roles."

No surprise with the former; the latter was an interesting choice. Zefross Jackson was an African American actor new to the Playhouse, and so far had been limited to small supporting roles. But I thought he had potential and knew Mother felt the same.

"Anyway," Miguel was saying, "your mother's waiting for you. And I'd like to lock up and get home . . . it's been a trying day."

He escorted me, with Sushi in my arms, out through the building and its aisles to the entrance, then stayed behind. He had a faulty garage door to tend to.

Mother was standing by our car, her face bathed in the security lighting and bearing a disagreeable expression, as the overcast night sky grumbled.

As I approached, she was grumbling too. "Some help *you* were! I could have used a little support."

"You seem to've done fine without me," I said, adding disingenuously, "and I think you'll have a production people will be talking about for years."

Mother took that the way I figured she would. "I feel the same! We must make interesting casting choices to keep up with changing times. So I forgive you, dear. Now, I want to check on our usually trusty janitor."

"Leon? Let's not bother with that. I'm sure he's all right." A few sprinkles from the sky fell on my face.

"The sooner we check," she said emphatically, "the sooner we get home." Then she strode to her side of the car.

Muttering, I climbed in behind the wheel and handed Sushi to her. Some days just didn't want to end.

Leon Jones lived about a ten-minute drive from the Playhouse, in a trailer Mother had found for him, making for an easy commute to his janitorial job.

Since I didn't know the way, she directed me along several gravel country roads, then down a pitted dirt lane that snaked through a heavily wooded area. By this time, the raindrops had evolved to a fine mist, and ground fog had begun creeping across the roadways, often obliterating them.

The ten-minute trip had turned into twenty when I finally pulled the C-Max up to a shabby-looking single-wide mobile home sitting in a clearing of tall pine trees, a propane tank squatting next to it like a prowler. No lights could be seen through partially drawn window shades.

"His truck is gone," Mother said, referring to Leon's battered Ford pickup.

"Then he's away somewhere," I said. "Let's go before this weather gets worse."

"Let me try him one more time," she said, cell phone in hand.

I had been staring at the darkened windows when I suddenly saw a flicker of light. The light seemed to pulse with the ringtone coming through Mother's phone.

"He won't answer you," I said, and told her why.

"Now that's odd," she said. "Who goes and leaves their cell phone behind?"

"Maybe he doesn't want to be bothered," I replied. Just as Mother sometimes left her cell behind when she wanted to investigate secretively.

"I'm going inside," she announced, reaching for her purse on the car floor.

Mother carried lockpicks in every purse she owned, like some women always make sure they have aspirin or lipstick along.

"So you're going to break in," I said.

"I'm the *sheriff,*" she announced, as if I hadn't heard that before. "I have probable cause."

"What cause?"

"Cause for worry."

"Is that a legal thing?"

She ignored that, got out, then ducked her head back in. "Come, I'll need you to hold the flashlight while I work my magic."

I sighed, turned off the car, and exited into the mist, Mother leading the way, Sushi trotting behind her, me bringing up the rear while keeping the flashlight's beam on the metal steps to trailer's door.

Soon, we three were inside, Mother quickly locating an overhead light.

To our left was the kitchen, composed of a dilapidated card table and plastic folding chairs, warped wooden cupboards, outdated appliances, and a sink filled with dirty dishes overseen by a dripping faucet.

To our right, the living room had a stained beige carpet, small flat-screen TV, worn brown couch, green recliner, and scarred coffee table with an ashtray that was filled, but not with the remains of cigarettes. At least not the commercial variety.

The air was heavy with a strong musky smell that reminded me of disturbed skunk. It permeated everywhere.

I said, "I never noticed Leon smelling of marijuana."

"I told him to make sure not to," Mother said, implying she knew of his pastime.

"You *do* know cannabis is illegal in this state, except for medical use."

She shrugged. "Perhaps he has a *condition.* Now make yourself useful."

"Doing what?"

Rather than say, Mother walked away, heading to the back of the mobile home.

I walked into the kitchen, where mail had

been collecting on the counter, and sifted through the stack, which was mostly junk mail and bills. But I found one item of interest — a brochure from a local auto dealer advertising new Ford trucks, with one particular model circled in red.

Did Leon have the kind of money for that? Even with a loan, the salary of the janitorial position at the Playhouse wouldn't cover a new truck's monthly payments. Of course, from the look of his digs, not much had been invested here. Maybe he'd built a nest egg.

Mother returned.

"His closet has been cleared out," she said. "And the bathroom cabinet is empty." She frowned. "I just don't understand it. Why would Leon skip and not tell me? After all I've done to help him."

Mother was clearly hurt. Justifiably so.

"Maybe he felt he was letting you down," I said. "And was too embarrassed to let you know he was quitting."

"I suppose." She sighed. "They say no good deed goes unpunished."

"Let's leave," I said. "This pot stench is giving me a headache." I gestured to Sushi, who was sprawled on the couch. "And heaven knows what it's doing to her."

"She does look a little docile."

I picked Sushi up, Mother doused the overhead light, and we got out of there.

After being subjected to fog inside the trailer, the fog outside was a welcome relief, the mist feeling good on my face.

Mother, having taken the flashlight, was lighting the way to the car when Sushi sprang from my arms, hit the ground running, and headed into the woods.

"What's gotten into her?" Mother asked.

"That's the second time this evening she's gotten away from me," I said. "I'm beginning to think I'll have to leave her at home after this . . . no matter what revenge she might wreak."

Suddenly, Sushi reappeared but held her ground at the edge of the forest.

"She's wants us to follow her," Mother said.

"I know that," I said warily, reminded of a few weeks ago, when we were in an old cemetery in Antiqua (*Antiques Ravin'*), where she had led me to a terrible discovery.

Sushi barked, then disappeared again.

This was what I got from watching old *Lassie* shows with her on my lap. Darling little devil doesn't miss anything.

We entered the woods, Mother trying to keep the beam on a moving Sushi, whose head could barely be seen above the thick ground fog creeping along with us, its white fingers swirling around our feet, as if trying to capture or trip us.

Suddenly I'd lost track of Sushi, so I called out. Her bark seemed to come from behind us.

We reversed course, Sushi's yapping increasing in volume and intensity with our every step, as if she were a Geiger counter delivering us to some buried treasure.

Only . . . I had a bad feeling that what was beneath the spot Sushi was now standing on, and pawing at, was not treasure at all.

Mother seemed to have come to the same conclusion. She said, "Dear, you'll need to go back to the car for the shovel."

Our trunk was a veritable mini-mart, with anything we might need should we ever be stranded.

I protested. "I'll never find my way there, let alone back."

She nodded. "Very well. Get me a thick stick — a piece of bark. *Anything* that I can use to scoop up dirt."

I faded back a step. "Mother, please. Call for backup."

Mother shook her head. "What if this is nothing but another dog's buried bone she's sniffed out? I'll look foolish."

Since when had that been a consideration?

She went on, "Also, it would be a waste of resources and taxpayer's money."

Since when did she care about *that,* either?

"All right," I said. "I'll find something . . . hand me the flashlight." She did, and I hunted nearby, then managed to pull a chunk of bark from a tree.

Mother took it and, knees cracking, knelt before the area that Sushi had marked, the fog parting at her presence as if by the force of her will and personality.

She looked like a child digging in a sand-box with a toy shovel.

After a while, Mother said, "I need more light, Brandy. Come closer."

"Do I have to?"

"Yes! You can keep your eyes closed."

Which was what I did.

The only sound in the forest was that of *swoosh,* as the tree bark went into the soil, and *plop,* as the dirt was cast aside.

Then came a moment of complete silence, followed by Mother's gasp.

My eyes still closed, I asked, "Is it . . . a body?"

"Yes, dear."

"Leon?"

"No, dear," she replied, with a little catch in her voice. "Someone I was not at all

142

expecting."

And I couldn't help it, I really couldn't. My eyes popped open.

And added to my mental album of dead faces I had seen since returning to Serenity and Mother, and a seemingly endless spate of murder investigations, was that of James "Jimmy" Sutter.

A Trash 'n' Treasurers Tip

If you have questions or concerns once your online purchase arrives, contact the dealer or auction site immediately. If a remedy exists, it may be time-sensitive. I once opened a package to make sure it was the correct item but failed to inspect it right away. By the time I discovered that the *Caddyshack* gopher's dance mechanism was broken, it was too late to return (it did play "I'm Alright," though).

Chapter Six:
In Which Vivian
Gets Up to Speed
and Brandy Makes
a Pit Stop

Vivian here.

I apologize for a momentary interruption in our story, but I feel strongly that I must complain about my participation so far in the writing of this book, which, in my opinion, has been negligible.

First, I had only a few paltry pages at the beginning of chapter 3 before Brandy took over — to pay the devil's daughter her due, she did allow me the Trash 'n' Treasures Tip at the conclusion — and, second, it wasn't until nearly halfway through the narrative that I have been allowed to directly participate in its creation. This is unacceptable, and I shall forthwith take it up with our editor.

(**Editor to Vivian:** May I remind you that your minimal participation in the writing of chapter 3 was due to your being ejected by the medical examiner from the autopsy room, when you failed to honor his requests that you were not to interrupt him?)

(**Vivian to Editor:** I need no reminder of that indignity, thank you. But the medical examiner needs to be reminded that I am the duly appointed sheriff of Serenity County, thank you very much.)

Anywho, she's *B-A-A-A-C-K!* And by "she" I mean *moi.* But before resuming my rightful position in the telling of this tale, I should like to thank all of the readers who snail-mailed, e-mailed, tweeted, and blogged your endorsement of my stance against the ill-usage of "no problem."

This misused phrase is mostly practiced by millennial waitstaff when asked to do something that is *part of their job,* such as refilling a customer's coffee cup. However, I recently received an even *more* inappropriate response to a request of mine.

Would you like me to explicate? I thought as much.

I was in our local drugstore acquiring a laxative (not that I needed one, but I do like to have such products on hand, just in case) when I spotted one of those Dr. Scholl's machines on which you step to map your feet and learn what particular insoles might be best slipped into your shoes. My results showed that I needed the CF 220, but the kiosk had sold out of that insert, so

I traversed the aisles until I found a young female employee, who was stocking the shampoo shelf. I politely asked her if she might check in that mysterious place known only as "in back" to see if there were, in fact, more 220s available.

Well.

She nodded and replied, "No worries."

As she started off, I asked, "Why? *Should* I be worried?"

The young woman glanced back and said, "Huh?"

And I said, "Why in heaven's name would I be worried about something as trivial as insoles?"

Her response, which I would characterize as sullen, was, "Do you want me to look or not?"

When I responded in the affirmative, the woman went away, then came back in a while saying she was sorry, but she couldn't find any. So I told her not to worry about it.

(**Editor to Vivian:** Could you pick this up where the previous chapter left off — *please.*)

(**Vivian to Editor:** No problem.)

Brandy's face had turned as white as the surrounding ground fog as she pointed to the deceased and very gray-looking Jimmy

146

Sutter, swaddled in a blanket. I, for one, was glad his eyes were closed, because had they been staring, it would have been most unsettling. Thank the Lord for small favors!

Brandy said, "But . . . but . . . he died in the fire."

I was still kneeling by the shallow grave, looking up at her. "Apparently not, dear."

"Then *who* did? Die? In the fire?"

I didn't answer that question (or was it three?), grappling with this surprising wrinkle myself. Although, to my credit, I must admit I'd had my suspicions that the badly burnt body I viewed in the autopsy room didn't resemble Jimmy exactly. I might have shared that thinking with you at the time, but then that would have spoiled the surprise, wouldn't it?

Brandy was asking, "Could it have been Leon?"

I held out my hand for assistance in rising, as my knees are not what they used to be. As my dear daughter complied, I said, "Possibly, but not likely, because our apparently faithless janitor is gone — as are his truck and clothes — implying he's skedaddled."

Brandy scratched her cheek. "If Leon is the one who killed Mr. Sutter, and buried him out here . . . what could be the reason?"

"Well, burying a dead body is as good a thing to do with one as any."

She looked as if she might scream, but she only asked, "But why *kill* your friend Jimmy?"

Having no answer for that either, I got out my cell and called Deputy Chen and filled him in, including directions to the trailer. Then I reached Chief Cassato, directly, and did the same. He said he'd contact forensics. Who were probably snuggled warm in their wee little beds, as midnight was fast approaching. (That last sentence was my observation, not the chief's, who was muttering something I couldn't quite pick up when he clicked off.)

Brandy looked tired, and frankly unnerved, to be in the late Jimmy's presence.

I said, "I think it might be best you go home, dear."

"Oh, no. And leave you here alone?"

"I'll be just fine."

"Really?"

"Deputy Chen will have no trouble finding me."

Grateful, she asked, "Do you want me to leave Sushi for company?"

"Not necessary."

"Okay. But I'll wait by the trailer until Deputy Chen arrives."

I nodded.

Brandy hesitated, looking from me to Jimmy and back again. "Call if you need me."

"I will, dear."

"You'll . . . be all right?"

"Yes, and I can use my cell light as a beacon. Go."

I handed Brandy the flashlight, and she and Sushi were soon swallowed up by the fog.

Dear reader, would you think ill of me if you knew that I wasn't particularly upset at finding Jimmy? Surprised, yes, but upset? No. And not because I was, or am, callous. This was a professional matter, and another opportunity to demonstrate to those who doubted my abilities as sheriff to find out how wrong they were. This body, an obvious homicide, had been discovered on my (as the chief of police put it) patch, putting me squarely in charge.

I returned to a sitting position next to Jimmy, to keep him company.

Now, like any good author, I would have preferred to share with you, at an earlier juncture, what we call backstory, re: my relationship with Jimmy. That would have enabled you to get to know him better, which would give his death more impact, perhaps tugging at your heartstrings (novice writers take note!). But I was never given an opportunity (Google "point of view") until my autopsy room account, which was cut short. I will do so now — even though it may be less effective in the telling at this point — because Jimmy deserves nothing less, and, you know . . . better late than never.

I was older than he . . . never mind by how much — that's on a need-to-know basis, and you don't need to know. Also, a smart woman protects her age just as she does her reputation. Suffice to say, Jimmy and I never attended school together. James Sutter came on my radar many years ago, when he protested the city council voting to demolish an entire downtown block of turn-of-the-nineteenth-century buildings.

These physical structures held many of my youthful memories: the red-brick three-story YWCA where I attended sock hops and played girls basketball; the Art Deco Paradise Theater, where in the back row of the sagging balcony, my first kiss was stolen (by me or my companion? that would be telling); the drugstore where friends would gather at the soda fountain, and play the jukebox; and Honest Abe's Used Car Emporium, where I purchased my first vehicle, a blue Rambler that died in the middle of an intersection right after I drove it off the lot.

And what did the city use this entire block for? A gold star to those of you who correctly guessed "a parking lot."

So the next time the council brought in a wrecking ball to destroy an architectural gem — our sadly now-gone Victorian-era library — I chained myself to its front door in protest and threw away the key. Only one other person joined me in protest, risking a jail sentence — one James Sutter. We became instant friends, and cofounded the Serenity Historical Preservation Society, gathering like-minded citizens to join us as watchdogs against further erosion of Serenity's historical heritage.

Was Jimmy rather more than a friend? A polite woman never kisses and tells (reputation-guarding, remember? I will say that it wasn't him in the Paradise balcony). I do admit that he once had asked me to accompany him to the altar, but I gently declined. I'd grown accustomed to my independence in widowhood, and a solid union cannot be built on old architecture alone.

I used the back of my hand to wipe my

cheeks, which had gotten damp from the fog.

In the distance, a faint siren wailed, growing louder with each passing second. Another siren joined in, until the shrill cacophony seemed almost upon me, before stopping abruptly somewhere in the near darkness.

Soon, a pair of flashlight beams were cutting through the forest, crisscrossing like lightsabers, and I shone my cell light toward them, like the Bat-Signal (too many pop culture references, do you think?). Then the two other beams came together, bathing me and Jimmy in one spotlight, and I looked up at Deputy Charles Chen and Chief Tony Cassato.

My deputy asked, "Sheriff, are you all right?"

"Yes. And Brandy?"

"I sent her home," the chief said. He nodded to the grave. "Are you sure that's James Sutter?"

"I am. We were well acquainted." I held my hand out, and Charles assisted me to my feet. For some reason Deputy Chen prefers not to be called "Charlie."

"Then who died in the fire?" the deputy asked, echoing Brandy.

I was brushing myself off. "That has yet

152

to be determined."

Tony asked, "How did you find the grave?"

"I didn't. Sushi did."

I explained that Leon's uncharacteristic absence from the audition tonight had led Brandy and me to check on him, only to find his truck and personal belongings M.I.A. I theorized aloud that a blanket taken from the marijuana-laced trailer had been used to wrap and then drag the body in, giving Sushi a scent to follow.

"Smart dog," Tony said. "I could use her on the K-9 unit."

His cell sounded. Forensics were on their way. Since the sheriff's department had no forensics, the Serenity police handled that for us.

Leaving Deputy Chen to guard the grave, Tony and I walked back through the woods in silence to meet the team.

Standing near the two squad cars, as their strobing lights turned our faces red then blue, Tony said, "Now that the Sheriff's Department is involved, you'll be needing an update on the mansion fire."

I tried not to look too smug; he was behaving in a professional manner, after all. "That's right. And the sooner the better — a meeting seems called for with you, the coroner, medical examiner, and fire marshal. Do you wish to organize it, or shall I?"

He shrugged. "Be my guest."

I took a step closer. "Let's call a truce, shall we? With two dead bodies, a missing janitor, and a suspicious fire, there's plenty of investigating to go around."

He granted me the tiniest of smiles. "I do prefer having you on board to you sneaking around."

"With all due respect," I said, "I do not sneak. There's never been sneaking. Not one single instance, sneaking-wise."

He grunted. "Not one wise instance, maybe. Just repeated ones. Often illegal in nature."

I put hands on hips. "Name one!"

"Just one?"

"All right, then — name as many as you like!"

"How much time do we have?"

"When?"

Another shrug; he seemed insufferably calm. "I could begin when first I met you, the time you came to my office *ostensibly* to welcome me as the new chief, then pretended to cough, asked for some water, and when I left the room to get you some, you rifled through my desk."

"That's not strictly true," I maintained. Then added, "I do admit to leaving my chair to look at the picture on the wall behind the desk, but —"

"There's a security cam in my office."

"What I *meant* by 'that's not *strictly* true' was that I really *did* have a cough."

He rubbed his chin, eyes looking up as if his memory were hovering. "Then there was the succession of dispatchers I had to fire for giving you confidential information after you bribed them with Godiva chocolates, parts in plays, and — my favorite — an autographed photo of George Clooney. By the way, was that really his signature?"

I shook my head. "Forged. That's not illegal, and do you really think someone who can't be trusted need be dealt with forthrightly?"

He grunted again. "Shall I move on to breaking and entering?"

My lips performed a modest Bronx cheer. "That was all *before* I became sheriff. I thought we were going to call a truce."

The chief's voice turned serious. "We are. But you have to understand that since you *are* sheriff, it's imperative that you go by the book. Otherwise, you could compromise these investigations — mine, yours, and ours."

I cocked my head. "I do believe, Chief Cassato, that this is the longest conversation we've ever had — and while it has not been entirely pleasant, I do think we've reached a professional understanding." I pointed a finger. "But I do *not* cop to sneaking."

A white utility van arrived with Serenity's two forensics specialists: Henderson, an overweight, world-weary veteran with salt-and-pepper hair, and Wilson, noticeably younger with a shaved head and flat nose.

The pair got out, gave us professional nods, circled the vehicle to the rear, then opened the back doors and began hauling out their equipment.

Having no desire to tromp back through the forest and compromise the area further, I informed the chief I wanted to take another look inside the mobile home but did not wish to disturb any potential evidence.

He gave me a nod of permission. "They won't get to that for a while."

I left the three men to their tasks.

Inside the trailer, a sudden weariness descended upon me — perhaps a delayed reaction to finding Jimmy — and I sought repose on the couch. Nice to have a peaceful moment to myself.

I'd been sitting there in quiet contemplation for a few minutes when a terrific explosion lifted me up off the sofa, then unceremoniously dumped me down again with a *whump!*

Next came a *whoosh!* as a fireball roared toward me from the rear of the trailer. I jumped to my feet, grateful for my stellar hip replacements; scrambled to the door; and hurtled myself out, where I dropped to the ground, then rolled away from the licking flames that had completely engulfed the mobile home. Its squat neighbor, the propane tank, had vanished.

I lay there, stunned, when suddenly an out-of-breath Tony was bending over me, asking me if I was hurt, to which I responded that I didn't really know.

Then the world faded to black.

Brandy's face came into focus.

"Where am I?" I asked.

"Hospital. Private room."

"*How* am I?"

"A mild concussion," she said. She summoned a supportive smile. "You seem determined to be burned to death. Or have you angered the god of fire?"

"I don't recall doing anything to offend Hephaestus."

Her eyes widened; she seemed impressed by my erudition.

"What happened, dear?" I asked. "Help me sit up."

Brandy adjusted the bed while speaking. "Seems the propane tank next to the trailer exploded."

"Good lord," I said, then wondered aloud, "Accidentally? Or intentionally?"

Brandy shook her head. "All I know is that you're alive, and I'm grateful for that. Things would be pretty dull without you."

My head was spinning — with thoughts, not general concussion-related dizziness — when Brandy put another thought in there.

"That vase you'd hoped to rescue at the Wentworth place?" she said. "It turned up online."

"Do you think it's *the* vase?"

"Sure looks like it. And each one of those things, that I've seen anyway, seems pretty distinctive."

"Where did you spot it?"

"On the website of an antiques shop in downtown Chicago — Clark Street Antiques."

"Satisfactory," I said. That was what Nero Wolfe said when Archie Goodwin delivered, and Brandy had.

"What are you going to do about it?" she asked. "Go there yourself, or contact the Chicago authorities?"

A third choice occurred to me, but I kept that to myself, for reasons that will become clear (but not to Brandy).

"I'm doing nothing at the moment, dear," I said, adding sternly, "and do keep this information about the vase just between us."

A knock on the doorjamb announced Tony, who strode in saying, "How's the patient?"

"See for yourself," Brandy said, rising from the chair. "I'm going to get some coffee — either of you want any?"

We both declined.

She slipped out, and Tony took her place in the bedside seat of honor.

"You up to answering some questions?" the chief asked.

"Of course."

"Before the explosion, did you hear a gunshot?"

"Why? Do you think that's what caused the tank to explode?"

"One possibility," he said.

I thought for a moment. "No, I don't recall a gun firing. But, then, I was at the opposite end of the trailer."

"Which was lucky for you."

"Quite. Anything salvageable of the trailer and/or its contents?"

The chief shook his head, then said,

"Luckily the fire was contained to the immediate area. Those woods could be raging about now." He paused. "We did find pieces of the propane tank, which we'll turn over to an explosives expert for possible determination of cause."

The room went quiet for a moment or two.

I said, "We need to have that departmental meeting this afternoon. And I need to be there."

Tony raised his eyebrows. "The doctor said you'd be here for another day."

"I have it from a higher authority that I'll be out by noon."

He smirked. "You're talking about either Jehovah or yourself. I'm guessing the latter."

I gave him my sweetest smile.

He sighed, and stood. "I'll arrange the meet, Sheriff."

As Tony was exiting, Brandy entered, Styrofoam cup in hand, and they exchanged brief words before he was gone.

I called her over.

"Get my clothes, dear."

"What, again?" the girl whined. "Can't I at least finish my coffee?"

"It's a to-go cup, darling girl. And it's time to go."

■ ■ ■ ■

The meeting was convened at the police station in the conference room shortly after one o'clock. On the table in front of us were yellow notepads and pens, along with bottles of water. Tony sat at the head of the oval-shaped table, yours truly to his right. Across from me was Coroner Hector Hornsby and, next to him, Medical Examiner Tom Peak, followed by Fire Marshal Stephen Nelson.

Tony said simply, "We need to bring Vivian up to speed." His eyes went to the fire marshal. "Stephen?"

The man, around forty, boyish-looking, with sandy hair and deep blue eyes, sat up straight and cleared his throat.

I put pen tip to pad.

"The source of Wentworth mansion fire remains undetermined," he said, "but is suspected to've started in either the front bedroom fireplace or the fireplace directly below in the sitting room. You see, Sheriff, because of the way the house had been built —"

I interrupted. "I do not require a lesson in Victorian architecture, young man. I'm aware that the structure had no fire walls between floors — that's why it went up like a box of matchsticks. What I want to know is what's being done to further the investigation."

To his credit, the fire marshal kept his composure, his unlined face showing only the slightest flush. "The state fire marshal is arriving tomorrow."

"Why not today?"

Stephen looked at Tony for help but didn't receive any.

"Because," the fire marshal said, "the insurance company has its own investigator there now."

"What?" I bellowed.

The man shifted uncomfortably in his chair, then summoned up some spine. "They have every right to examine the ruins, Sheriff."

"But surely," I said, "not until *after* the state investigators conclude their on-site examination."

The fire marshal found some more backbone. "State couldn't get here until tomorrow, and every day that passes wastes time, especially with rain in the forecast."

I said unhappily, "Well, what's done is done."

Stephen, his mouth a thin line, sat back in his chair.

"What do you have for me, Hector?" I

asked. One does not have to sit at the head of a table to dominate it. Was there any doubt?

The coroner looked at Tony, who gave him a nod.

The balding, bespectacled man shuffled papers in front of him. "First, I have the external autopsy report on the body found in the Wentworth fire. . . ."

I waved a dismissive hand. "Already have that."

His eyes narrowed behind the spectacles. "How?"

"Not pertinent. What else?"

More papers shuffled. "I also have the external report conducted early this morning on the body discovered in the woods."

"You didn't wait for me?" I protested.

The coroner shrugged. "You were in the hospital."

Tom, more diplomatic, replied, "Sheriff, the examination couldn't wait. The man was getting . . . ripe."

Still, I gave the medical examiner my finest glare.

Hector began passing out copies of the report as he spoke. "The body is that of James Sutter, previously thought to be the person who died in the fire, now referred to as John Doe."

"*Which* I most likely could have told you," I said, "*if* I'd been allowed to stay through Mr. Doe's autopsy, as is my right as sheriff."

That hung in the air for a moment before Hector continued.

He said, "Mr. Sutter died from a blow to the back of the skull, as had Mr. Doe."

I glanced at the one-page report before tossing it aside. "This is useless — weight, height, hair color — where's the estimated time of death?"

Hector's response was condescending. "Sheriff, this is the *external* — or preliminary — report Tom conducted."

"I'm aware of that," I snapped. "When will the *internal* report be available?"

Tom answered. "That's in the hands of the University of Iowa Hospital, who will conduct that. They have three pathologists on staff with better equipment than what's available to us."

I nodded, then said, "I assume there'll be another look at John Doe to try to identify him."

Hector and Tom exchanged glances.

"What?" I asked.

Hector, avoiding my eyes, said, "I'm afraid that's not possible."

I set my pen down. "Let me guess. John Doe has been cremated."

Hector's shrug was apologetic. "Gavin Sutter wanted to go ahead with the funeral, and I saw no need to refuse him." The coroner added, lamely, "And, of course, this new wrinkle wasn't known at the time."

I drummed my fingers on the table, showing my displeasure.

Tom said, "I did take various tissue samples from John Doe, so we do have DNA."

"Thank you," I said, "for that much."

Tony picked up the mantle. "I suggest we look at the possibility that John Doe could be the absent Leon Jones — or at least, not rule that out." He looked at me. "Even though Leon's mobile home was destroyed, forensics might be able to collect DNA from his workplace at the Playhouse. Sheriff?"

"He had a closet where he kept some personal things," I said, nodding. "Good thinking. It's a start."

Tony continued. "And I'll see what medical records I can obtain from the prison where he did time."

The meeting felt as if it was winding down, but I wasn't finished yet.

I addressed Tom. "Getting back to James Sutter — why is there no estimated time of death given on the external you conducted twelve hours ago?"

"There never is."

"Not even a guestimate?"

"I prefer not to make 'guestimates,'" he responded. "Too many variables. The fact is, Sheriff, unless the end of life is witnessed, all that can be known for a certainty is that the time of death falls somewhere between when the person in question was last seen and when the body is found." He paused. "But I *can* tell you that rigor mortis had completely disappeared."

"Thirty-six hours after death," I said.

That impressed them.

I said, "So, if I found Jimmy . . . er . . . Mr. Sutter around midnight last night, and saw him last at five p.m. on Monday, the total of hours between would be . . ." I did the math on the pad. "Fifty-five hours. And fifty-five minus thirty-six is nineteen hours." More scribbling. "Which means Mr. Sutter was killed sometime between five Monday afternoon and noon on Tuesday."

Tom nodded. "That would be a fairly reasonable —"

"Guestimate?" I said.

He smiled just a little. "Call it an esti-mate."

I held his eyes. "What else can be learned from the internal autopsy that might narrow the time further?"

"Perhaps something regarding contents of

166

the stomach, the level of vitreous potassium, possibly corneal cloudiness. All of those could help."

I swiveled to Tony. "You have a BOLO out on Leon and his truck?"

The chief nodded. "Already done." He glanced around. "Anything more? From anyone?"

There wasn't.

Chairs were pushed back.

While Hector, Tom, and Stephen beat a hasty retreat, Tony and I lingered.

"Chief, I'd like to make inquiries about who else might have either seen or spoken to Mr. Sutter after I did. Any problem with that?"

"No," the chief said. "Just keep me informed so we're not covering the same ground." He paused. "Kind of rough on them, weren't you?"

I arched an eyebrow. "You disapprove?"

A slight softening of the steel-gray eyes told me he didn't.

"But you *do* have to work with them," he said. "I understand you're schooling them in respecting you and your office. And I'm fine with that. But you may wish to moderate your interaction with these public servants, starting next time."

I smiled. "Understood. You know, whenever I direct a play with a new cast, I find a moment early on to blow my gasket. After that, I'm helpful and polite and, really, very nice. But the actors always know what Vivian Borne is capable of."

He grunted. "That's more than I can say."

VIVIAN'S TRASH 'N' TREASURES TIP
The condition of an item is imperative. The online description should list the age, period, style, provenance, any damage or restoration that has been done, and finally a guarantee that the antique it is not a replica. Of course, if you're overly persnickety, you may get an e-mail from the seller saying that the item has been sold to someone else.

Chapter Seven:
In Which Vivian
Makes a Call
and Jake Holds the Line

Hi. My name is Jake, and I just turned fourteen. Brandy is my mom, and Vivian is my grandmother. I live with my dad and stepmom in a Chicago suburb called Naperville. He's an investment banker, and she's a pediatrician. They have hard jobs so I try to stay out of trouble, but sometimes I can't help it, like now.

Some of you may remember me, and how I got involved in one of Grandma's cases when I was twelve and visiting on fall break. Dad was *furious* after he found out that I got put in danger, and he banned me from seeing Grandma and Mom for a while. But then he got over it, or forgot about the ban, or whatever, because I've been back to Serenity many times since.

You've probably already guessed that Grandma wants me to do something for her today, which is Friday, and you may even have guessed what that something might be, and how that means I'm going to have to skip school.

I'm in eighth grade at Jefferson Middle School. That's a public school. I used to go to a private one, but I won't say which, because I did like some of the teachers there and don't want to make them look bad. But just the same, I didn't like it. In fact, I ran away, but I won't go into that.

Anyway, I skipped school before by saying I was sick, like when I first got Red Dead Redemption, a video game set in the Wild West that's kind of violent but has really cool graphics. But with a stepmom who's a doctor, I can't pull that very often and hope to get away with it.

After the divorce, when I was eleven, things got really tense between Mom and Dad. Started when she used bad judgment at her ten-year high school reunion. I probably shouldn't even know about that, but she talks about it in her books and I've read those.

Anyway, now they get along okay for divorced parents. Have to admit, sometimes I wish I lived with Mom and Grandma, because I miss them, and things are never dull around where they live. But then I'd be missing my dad, and he and I do get along better than most. So what's a kid supposed to do?

What else do you need to know?

Let's see. Oh, maybe I should have said this earlier, but when you picture me, I take after my mom. I'm a little on the short side, but expect to make up for that soon (Dad says he had a growth spurt around my age), and I have blond hair, like Mom, but blue eyes, not brown like hers. Our noses are pretty much alike.

At times, when I'm with Mom, I feel like she's studying me like I was a germ under a microscope or something. I know she's worried I might get what Grandma has, which is a mental thing called bipolar, meaning I would have to take medication . . . but so far I feel I'm all right in my upstairs. Anyway, what's wrong with being a little out there? At least Grandma's not boring.

Well, that's enough about me to get you by.

Last night, after dinner, Grandma texted me, asking how I was doing, and I texted her back some school stuff, like I have a part in the school's winter play. Then she came back, saying how proud she is of me and how theater must be in my blood. She signed off with "I love you more than the sun and the moon and the stars," which is a code for me to call her later in secret.

I had argued that the code ought to be something simple, like "later, gator," but she said I won't have trouble remembering the sun and the moon and the stars, and I guess she's right, even if it does make me cringe every time I see it.

Anyway, after my folks went to bed and their light went out, I called Grandma, and we had a whispered conversation while she told me what happened recently in Serenity.

At first, it was really disturbing hearing how she'd almost died in a fire, and I about lost it when she said she almost died *again,* getting blown up in a trailer! But that's Grandma. Then she gave me the really cool news that there had been two murders in Serenity. I know that sounds bad. But what made it cool is that she asked me to help her with some investigating.

This has happened before, murders in Serenity and Grandma asking for my help. Usually that means computer stuff, but this time she wanted me to go out and do some "fieldwork." I thought this time she really had lost her marbles, talking about farming or something, until she explained that what she meant was that I was supposed to check out some vase in an antiques store in downtown Chicago. She gave me the information, and told me what to say and ask, and also sent me a picture of this wack-looking vase. Also, if I felt in danger, she said I had to promise to bail.

After that, I had some trouble getting to sleep.

The next morning, when Dad and my stepmom were getting ready for work, I was in my bathroom, pretending to vomit, really loud. Hey, theater is in my blood, remember? And when I came out groaning and wiping my mouth with a hand towel, my dad and stepmom were right there, looking concerned. Obviously, I knew I wouldn't have a temperature, so I said my stomach hurt and I felt dizzy. They accepted that, even my doctor stepmom, and agreed I should stay home. I told them I'd send a text now and then about how I was feeling.

And that was that.

I stayed in bed for half an hour after they'd gone, in case one of them came back because they forgot something, like a brief-case or work notes or whatever, then I got dressed, gathered a few things in my back-pack, and grabbed my jacket.

Getting into the Loop is no easy jaunt from Naperville, and involves walking and busses and trains, and all that could take hours. I had some cash saved up for the new

Apple iPhone XR, and, knowing Grandma would pay me back, pocketed that and called a cab. My dad has an Uber account I can use for emergencies, but, yeah, then he'd find out. This needed to be a "stealth mission," a phrase Grandma used from time to time.

Fifty-some minutes later I got dropped off at the corner of Van Buren and Clark, just about the point where the Loop was starting to go a little sketchy. From there I walked another block south to Clark Street Antiques.

The store seemed okay from the outside, certainly better than the others around it (pizza place, pawn shop), and there were some real nice-looking antiques displayed in the big window that had bars on it.

I went on inside, where a buzzer buzzed to announce me, and stood looking around. I'd helped out at Grandma's Trash 'n' Treasures shop before, but the stuff in here was way more expensive, fancy old furniture and stuff, so I wasn't sure if I could pull this off.

There was a long glass counter to the right, full of small items like jewelry and whatnot, and a man was behind it. Once, when Grandma was trying to educate me about good movies, she showed me one in black and white called *Laura*. Anyway, in the film there was a snooty character who carried a cane and wore a hat and was in love with this Laura, and this man turned out to be the bad guy, who hid the murder weapon that was a shotgun in the grandfather clock. Oh, I hope I didn't just ruin that movie for anybody! I should have said "Spoiler Alert" first. But, anyway, that's who this man behind the glass counter reminded me of.

He looked down his nose and asked, real snooty, "*Something* I can help you with, young man?" He kind of talked through his nose, too.

I said, "I was hoping to find something for my grandmother. She loves just about anything antique."

He regarded me like I was some dirt that blew in, which only made me want to succeed more.

"I fear my inventory may be well above what you could afford," he intoned. (Using "said" gets monotonous. I hear real writers mix it up, so I'll try to do that.)

I moved toward the counter and flashed my cash. "Oh, I've *got* money."

The man thawed just a little. "Well . . . there *may* be a few things in the back."

That's when I spotted the vase behind him

175

on a shelf in a locked case.

"What about *that*?" I asked, pointing, making my eyes big and bright like Sushi's when I held a treat over her head. "My grandma just *loves* vases."

He raised his chin and snorted. "Congratulations, young man. You've managed to select one of the most expensive items in my shop."

I let my jaw drop. "What? That ugly thing?"

"Young man, *that* ugly thing is priced at one hundred thousand dollars. And a bargain at that."

What a big liar. Grandma had said seventy gee's, tops.

I shook my head. "You gotta be joking."

"Have you by chance ever heard of Louis Comfort Tiffany?"

"Ah . . ." I looked upward, like my eyes were trying to see inside my brain for the answer. "Didn't he make beautiful glass and jewelry and stuff?"

"Well, that's right." The man seemed a little surprised. Maybe even pleased.

"Then why would a guy as good at it as this Tiffany make *that* thing? I just pointed it out 'cause it's a vase, and Grandma's into old vases, and that sure is one."

"Because it's *art,* young man. And that

vase is beautiful . . . to those who can *appreciate* art."

"Valuable, huh? Rare?"

"Yes and yes."

"How did you land it, anyway?"

I may have just jinxed things, because he didn't answer and his eyes narrowed. "What's your name, young man?"

"Kyle Townsend." That was the fake name on the I.D. I carry, with a fake age of eighteen.

(**Note to Editor from Jake:** Do you think maybe we could skip that last sentence so I don't get into trouble? The I.D.'s only to get me into R-rated movies because my stepmom doesn't go for me seeing stuff like *Halloween* and *It*.)

(**Note to Jake from Editor:** Why not leave it in? You're going to be in trouble enough for the rest of this chapter.)

"And you are?" I asked the clerk.

He handed me a card, which I took and read out loud: "Mr. Percival Feddick, Esquire, Fine Antiques."

That sounded like *he* was a fine antique. Plus a pompous moron.

"Pleased to meet you," I said, and stuck out a hand, which he reluctantly shook. It felt cold and clammy, like a lunch meat package in the fridge.

177

I pressed again. "So how *did* you get that Tiffany vase? If it's so rare and all." When again I got no answer, I said, "Some high-priced auction place, I suppose."

"Noooo," he droned. "In such a case, I might well end up paying too much for it, and couldn't make a profit."

"Oh yeah, sure. Too much competition drives the price up." I guessed again. "Then someone who owned the thing musta needed money and brought it in to sell."

He was losing patience with me. "Mr. Townsend, don't you have a home? Somewhere to be? Isn't this a *school* day?"

Looking dejected, I whined, "How's a kid supposed to learn anything if adults won't explain things to them? Never mind school — teach me about this, now. You're an expert."

That approach usually works, and it did this time.

"Very well," Percival Feddick Esquire sighed. "Yes. Someone brought it in."

I perked up. "And then you bought it, for a lot less than it was worth, right?"

He nodded. "Most sellers understand that this is a business and that we cannot *stay* in business unless there is a margin of profit. And such sellers accept a reduction in their expectations. Yes. Of course. Now . . ."

"How do you know something isn't *stolen*? And that *that's* why the seller lets it go cheap?"

His lips pursed for a second. "Because I always check the police database of stolen merchandise before I buy *anything* — especially something as valuable as that vase."

"What else do you do to make sure it isn't hot?"

The world "hot" made his eyebrows go up. "I always ask the seller for provenance."

"What *about* Rhode Island?" I couldn't resist.

"Not *Providence,* Mr. Townsend, *provenance.*"

"What's that?" I asked eagerly, as if any morsel of information was just fascinating. I knew darn well what that word meant. Grandma had a way of making the provenance of something sound more interesting than it really was.

Feddick Esquire was saying, "It's a written history of the item, or, at the very least, information as to where the seller obtained the piece. A document to that effect is what I have in the instance of this vase."

"Wow. Can I see?"

He shrugged, ducked down behind the glass counter, and came back with a thick black binder. He opened the binder and turned it around to face me.

I thumbed through the plastic sleeves protecting various letters from sellers. Some were pretty formal, typed with signatures and even stamps of banks, while others were just handwritten notes.

Mr. Feddick swiveled the binder back, and closed it, having come to the end of his patience with me.

But I had seen what I needed to — the handwritten letter that went with the vase, and the name of Alek Wozniak, plus his address.

I thanked Feddick, wandered to the back of the store, looked for something small, spotted a pair of silver salt-and-pepper shakers for forty dollars, and took my purchase to the front.

Just to mess with him, I asked for the provenance paper on the shakers, and it turned out there wasn't one. But I took the things anyway, paying him. As a paying customer, I wouldn't leave him with any suspicions. He wrapped the items and put them in a sack, and I left.

Outside, I checked my phone and saw I'd missed two texts. One was from Dad, the other from Grandma, each asking how I was doing. To both I texted I was "doing all right," which they'd interpret each in their own way.

I called for a cab to take me to the address on the provenance doc, which turned out to be on the west side of Chicago near Pulaski Park. I went there once on a school trip to see the fieldhouse that was built by Jens Jensen, whose name I'd remembered because Grandma's used to be Jensen before she got married way back when.

I got dropped off at a strip mall, at a store called Best in the Biz, which I didn't understand because that name wasn't part of the address I'd seen. But this *was* the address. Am I clear? Best in the Biz was a place where you could photocopy stuff and mail packages.

I went inside the place, which was kind of small, and when I saw the rows of mailboxes just to the right, I figured out that the number fifty-seven after the street address was not an apartment, like I'd thought, but where this Alek Wozniak picked up his mail. You could see through little glass slots into each box, and number fifty-seven had some mail in it, so maybe he hadn't picked today's up yet.

To the left were some computer stations, and a little work area with a couple of chairs, and that's where I thought I'd hang out waiting to see if the guy showed. But

181

first I needed to make sure I didn't cause any alarm by hanging around for who knows how long.

There were two people behind the counter, a man and woman, and I picked the woman because she was younger and might be easier to deal with. She wasn't busy, so I approached her and asked politely if it would be okay if I used the little work area to do some homework while I waited for my mom, who was held up at a doctor's appointment because the doctor was behind schedule. The whole time I was smiling shyly and kind of batting my eyelashes. That last one sounds sickening, but Mom has these long, pretty eyelashes and can get away with murder with guys when she does that. She says I have her eyes, so maybe it would work, too, on the opposite sex.

Seemed to, because the young woman smiled back and said, "No problem."

I went over to the worktable and got settled in on a chair, facing the rows of mailboxes, making sure that I had a good view of number fifty-seven. Then I got into my backpack and took out a schoolbook and some paper, because I really did have algebra to do.

Half an hour crawled by, and a few people had come in and gotten their mail, but not from the box I'd been watching.

I'd finished the algebra and was really getting bored with this part of investigating. I thought about playing *Fortnite* on my phone, but figured it might be too distracting, so I checked the menu to see if one of my friends was playing, and Brad was, so I opted to spectate him play, which means watch him do that. (Not him personally, but the moves he was doing in the game. I know, crazy.)

Suddenly a man came in, went directly to mailbox fifty-seven, stuck a key in, pulled out some letters, shut the box, pulled out the key, and left. It happened so fast that I didn't get much of a look at a guy who was probably Alek Wozniak. About all I got was he was husky and wearing a red jacket with the Cubs logo on the back. That part was lucky for me. It would make him easy to follow, unless a whole lot of Cubs fans were out there walking around.

Quickly, I packed my stuff up, smiled at the young woman who'd given me permission to hang around, got a smile and wave back, and rushed out on the sidewalk to see which way the Cubs jacket guy had gone. I saw him right away, up the street. Not another obvious Cubs fan in sight. He was walking fast, and I had to jog to keep up.

After a couple of blocks, the Cubs jacket guy entered a restaurant. I slowed down so I wouldn't be right on his heels, and then kind of sauntered inside of what turned out to be a Polish bakery and diner.

The first thing to greet me was a *long* glass case filled with pastries, like cakes and pies and cookies, and other stuff I didn't know the names of, but they sure looked good. I guess you can get pretty hungry working surveillance.

I headed toward the back where the restaurant section was, the glass case changing to deli-type food. I hadn't had anything to eat but a Pop-Tart this morning, not even toasted, and it was now about three o'clock, and I was really starving!

The eating area was about a dozen tables with red-and-white checkered plastic cloths, also some booths along one wall. There were a few other people besides me. Two guys were having coffee and arguing over football, and a little kid and his mother were eating cake. That cake looked pretty good.

But no red Cubs jacket.

Had Wozniak been tipped off by Feddick about some kid asking questions? Had he then tagged me in the mailbox place, ducked in here, and slipped out the back?

A voice behind me asked, "Are you just

going to stand there gawking? Or do you want something to eat?"

I turned and faced a blond waitress with dark roots, too much make-up, too much jewelry, a low-cut white blouse, and a tight black skirt. She was older than my mom, but not as old as grandma.

"Ah . . . I am going to have something to eat," I said, and took the nearest table.

"Good choice." She handed me a menu the size of suitcase, but I was still able to quickly make up my mind before she could leave.

"Give me a Coke, a cup of chicken dumpling soup, and a rare burger with cheese and onion and mustard."

She raised a thinly drawn eyebrow. "Polish burgers come one way. And rare's not it."

". . . Okay. However it comes is fine."

Then she was gone, leaving behind a sickly sweet scent of perfume.

I was sitting there wondering if I should have done something different when I tailed that guy. Had I screwed up somehow? Then the swinging door to the kitchen opened and a burly guy in white shirt and black pants came through tying a white bib apron around his middle, like he just got to work. He didn't look at me, instead focused on bussing a table, putting dirty dishes in a plastic tub, which gave me a chance to study the guy.

He wasn't a young man, but not old either. His hair was dark, almost black, slicked back. He had a high forehead, a long straight nose, not much of a mouth. His cheeks were rough, like the surface of the moon. Maybe he had a bad case of zits when he was my age.

The waitress was back with a tray of my food.

"Gee, what kept you?" I teased, hoping she might be of some use.

"What's your name, hon?" she asked.

I smiled. "Kyle. What's yours?"

"Hannah. Haven't seen you in here before."

"No. I'm from Naperville. Originally, I'm from a little town in Iowa, called Serenity."

She frowned in thought. "Serenity . . . where have I heard that before? Oh, yeah!"

The top half of her swiveled to the guy who was now wiping down the table he'd just bussed. "Hey, Alek! Don't you know someone from Serenity, Iowa?"

He stopped wiping and just stared at her.

I jumped in. Smiling. Friendly. "Be glad to say 'hi' for you," I said to him.

"Never heard of it," Alek said.

"I'm sure you mentioned —" Hannah said, but got cut off.

"I *said* I never heard of the place." He picked up the plastic tub and disappeared through the push door.

"Well, that was weird," I said to Hannah.

Hoping to pry a little more out of her, I asked, "Did Alek ever mention somebody's name? A him or a her?"

"Forget it," she said, not as friendly now. "I was wrong."

In fact, Hannah seemed a little scared now. I must have pressed too hard.

She lowered her voice. "You should eat and get out of here. Maybe don't come back."

"Oh, okay. Thanks."

Hannah just nodded. She was scared, all right. Not for herself, but me.

She left my ticket on the table.

I wolfed down the food. The burger was like meatloaf in a bun, but really good. I left cash on top of the ticket, including a good tip, slung my backpack on, and made tracks.

Out on the sidewalk, I was walking, staring at my phone, trying to call for a cab, when Alek was right in front of me. Like a wall I almost ran into.

"Who are you?" he asked quietly, which made him seem even more threatening.

Still, I felt relatively safe with traffic gliding by on the street and pedestrians passing on the sidewalk. So I went on defense. "What's it to you?"

"You were in that mailbox place."

I narrowed my eyes. "Yeah, doing homework. So what?"

"You followed me."

I smirked. "What for? I don't even know you. I wanted something to eat. You work there. Small world. Now stop stalking me or I'll call the police."

Wozniak backed off a little but pointed a thick finger at me. "This isn't your neighborhood. Don't come back."

"Don't worry. I wasn't planning to."

And I stepped around him.

Feeling his eyes burning holes in my back, I kept walking. I spotted a roaming cab and hailed it down.

I had the driver take me to the nearest shopping mall, where I got another cab for the ride home.

But it was rush hour traffic now, and the going was slow, and I was sweating bullets I wouldn't beat my stepmom home. She always got there before Dad.

Finally, the cab turned down my street, and I figured I was home free till I noticed the car directly in front of us was exactly like my stepmom's Lexus. There was a good reason for that. It *was* her Lexus, because I recognized the license plate.

The cab was just passing a side street when I yelled to the driver to turn there, then another turn put me somewhere behind my house.

Throwing some bills at him, I jumped out.

I ran between two homes, vaulted a wooden fence, tripped over a kid's bike, scaled someone else's chain-link fence, got chased by their dog, reached our fence, and flung myself over it. I dashed around the pool, dodged the hot tub, jumped over patio furniture, and reached the deck. Then I stood on its railing, pulled myself up onto the roof of the four-seasons room, clambered along its slope to my bedroom window, opened it, and tumbled inside. (Maybe I'd done this before.)

Below, I heard the front door slam shut and my stepmom call out, "Jake, honey . . . I'm home!" Her footsteps sounded on the wooden stairs. Like a firing squad marching to do their duty.

I picked myself up, tore off my backpack and jacket, stripped down to my T-shirt and boxers, and dove into bed just before my door opened.

Pretending to wake up, I garbled, "What?

189

Who? . . . Oh, hello."

"How are you feeling?"

"I'm not sure. . . ."

"Well, let's have a look." She pulled back the covers. "Oh, my . . . you're sopping wet! You must've had a fever." She felt my forehead. "But it's broken now."

If this was a movie, here's where I'd look at the camera and wink. Ferris Bueller had nothing on me.

"Are you hungry?" she asked.

"Not really," I answered. Not after bolting down that Polish meal I wasn't.

"What about some hot chocolate with marshmallows?" she asked.

But always room for that!

"That sounds really good," I said pitifully. "Thanks."

She nodded. "All right. I have to make a few phone calls first, and then I'll be up with it."

"Okay."

After the door closed, I let out a big sigh of relief.

I got up and retrieved my cell phone from my jeans, then sat on the edge of the bed.

"Grandma? Yeah, it's me, Jake. I'm back home."

The problem with investigating for Grandma was that she wanted to know every single solitary little detail of what had happened. That took a while — she even asked what I ate at the Polish diner.

"You did splendidly," Grandma said. "Much better than I could have."

That was a real compliment coming from her.

But I didn't think I'd done so good.

"Grandma, you *know* they're suspicious now. That vase and provenance note are gonna disappear from the antique store, Alek Wozniak will have his mail go somewhere else, and maybe change jobs."

"Dearest," she said. "That doesn't matter. You found the loose thread of yarn that will eventually unravel the entire sweater."

"I could try to talk to that Hannah again."

"No, dear." She was whispering now; Mom must've been around. "I've already put you in more danger than I ever intended."

"Well, okay. But Grandma?"

"Yes, dear?"

"You need to be careful yourself. Because that Alek Wozniak? He's not a nice man."

My door opened, and I raised my voice as a signal to her. "Yeah, I'm feeling better, Grandma. Probably go back to school tomorrow. . . . No, I won't get behind on my studies. . . . Yes, I'm staying hydrated. . . .

No, I won't get constipated." I looked at my stepmom and rolled my eyes. "Well, I'm gonna go back to sleep now. . . . Okay, I will. Say 'hi' to Mom and tell her I'll call her later. Bye."

All the while I was going through that phony conversation, Grandma was giggling on the other end of the line.

"She means well," my stepmom said with a smile, and handed me a mug of hot chocolate brimming with gooey marshmallows.

One final thing before I sign off, and this is just for kids with cell phones, so if you're not one (a kid, not a cell phone), you don't have to read on. In fact, it's probably best if you don't. So.

Every once in a while, I leave my phone lying around out in the open so my dad and stepmom can get a look at it — there's no password on mine, just a swipe to get in, which was the deal for them to buy me the iPhone SE. (And why I've been saving up for my own iPhone XR, with password.)

You can't blame parents for worrying and spying, because they probably remember all the bad stuff they did when *they* were our age. So go ahead and take the free phone offer. You can always delete all e-mails and texts and photos and tweets and other things that could make them crazy. Crazier. (And then hang on to that birthday and Christmas money.)

One suggestion? If you have a code that means something special from someone, make sure it's not lame like the sun and moon and the stars. Although I bet you'll remember that, won't you?

JAKE'S TRASH 'N' TREASURES TIP
The internet is a great place to get rid of any of your stuff that you're tired of and that takes up space in your room. I use Craigslist, and so far haven't been stiffed. There are even "safe zones" where you can meet a buyer to make the exchange, which says you're both legit. Also, then you get to buy new stuff with the money and fill your room back up.

CHAPTER EIGHT:
IN WHICH VIVIAN
BARKS UP THE WRONG TREE
AND BRANDY GOES
OUT ON A LIMB

Friday morning, Mother was up bright-eyed and bushy-tailed, and chomping at the bit (to mix metaphors), to begin questioning anyone who might have seen or talked to James Sutter from Monday evening through midday Tuesday. The focus would be on individuals with a connection to the mansion, her list including Gavin Sutter, Evelyn Snydacker, Benjamin Wentworth, and Cliff Reed.

Since she wanted to conduct her interviews not by phone but in person, to better gauge people's reactions to her questions, I was once again Mother's deputy/chauffeur. Joe Lange was called up for duty to look after the antiques shop — and Sushi — for the duration.

Leaving directly from home, we took the C-Max, Mother in her jumpsuit uniform with a tan windbreaker, me in jeans and a sweater. I had managed to resist any sort of uniform in my ex-officio role.

Our first stop was Gavin Sutter, who lived with his wife, Sarah, in a modest ranch home in a subdivision called Stoneybrook that had once been one of Serenity's most desirable neighborhoods thirty years ago and was still "nothing to turn your nose up at" (as Mother put it). He worked in management at the electric company, and Sarah subcontracted from home as a CPA; they had a daughter, Heather, who attended college out of state.

All of this was shared with me by Mother on the way. She must have cleared our visit with Gavin through his wife, because Sarah met us at the door, saying, "You won't keep him long, will you? We have an appointment with the funeral director — *again.*"

Sarah was a tall brunette with her hair pinned up, attractive even without makeup. She wore a tan sweater with gold necklace, brown tailored slacks, and brown socks sans shoes, and she was clearly frazzled.

I wondered if we were supposed to remove our shoes, too, but our hostess said nothing about that before ushering us into a formal living room, tastefully appointed if a bit bland.

Gavin was seated in an overstuffed armchair. He rose as we entered. He wore a navy V-neck sweater over an open-collared light blue shirt with gray slacks. He, too, was in his stocking feet, which I now figured was a practice born of the light beige carpet. It somehow brought immediately to mind this morning, when Sushi's long leash got wound around a bush in our backyard and I had to step through the fertilizer minefield to free her.

As Mother and I followed his gesture to occupy the couch, some back and forth between Sarah and her husband transpired. Did he want anything? No, he didn't. Coffee? No, thank you, darling. I would have loved a cup of joe, but no offer came and the wife departed. In her current state, caffeine wouldn't have been a good idea, if that was what she was off to acquire for herself.

Gavin sat forward, staring at the hands in his lap before meeting Mother's eyes.

"Sheriff, I owe you an apology," he said. "I behaved badly at the crematorium."

"Tut-tut," Mother responded, with a wave of her hand. "You were understandably overwrought, and who wouldn't be? We'll hear no more about it."

But I could tell she was pleased by his apology. Like most people who rarely offer apologies, Mother relished those she received.

Gavin went on: "And as it turned out, you were right to confiscate the body, which I had been told was that of my stepfather." He sighed. "If only I hadn't insisted the funeral go forward so quickly, Heather wouldn't have had to rush home just in time to see some unknown stranger's ashes put in the family vault!" He shook his head slowly. "Now we have to go through all of that again."

"However," Mother said, "this time the service and burial will be for the *actual* dearly departed."

Gavin sucked in some air. "Oh! I didn't mean to sound ungrateful, Sheriff. Thank God you found James. The *real* James." He shuddered. "To think that his final resting place might otherwise have been a shallow grave in the woods somewhere is . . . really, just unbearable."

"Happy to help," Mother said.

Our host frowned. "I heard you were in the hospital after an explosion of some kind? That very same night?"

"Yes, shortly after the discovery of your stepfather's body. A propane tank, dear, on the property where he was found."

It took more than one measly exploding propane tank to stop Vivian Borne.

She continued: "But I'm not here to

discuss that. And, and as you can see, I'm quite all right."

"Of course," Gavin said, taken slightly aback by Mother's sudden curtness. "Why *are* you here?"

Mother removed a small notepad and pen from a zipper pocket of her jumpsuit. "I have a few routine questions. I'll make it brief, since you've been put through this loss twice."

"I appreciate that," he said.

"When did you last speak to your stepfather?"

"You mean, the *very* last time?"

"Please."

"Well," Gavin said slowly, and he paused to mull the question. "I'm not exactly sure."

Mother prompted, "The day of the fire?"

"No."

"A few days before perhaps?"

A shake of his head.

"A few weeks, then?"

No reaction now.

"Months?"

Gavin cleared his throat. "If I might be frank . . ."

"I insist you be."

"My stepfather and I hadn't been on speaking terms for some time."

"And why would that be?" Mother asked bluntly.

He shifted in the armchair, clearly uncomfortable despite its generous padding, and when Gavin finally spoke, his voice was soft — any softer, he'd have been hard to make out at all.

"It was no one thing," he said, "no argument, certainly no shouting match. More a gradual thing, our falling out. You may already know that I cosigned the mortgage on that mansion, so James could buy it. This was just before the housing bubble burst."

Tired of sitting on the sidelines, particularly with no coffee, I said, "Then suddenly the Wentworth mansion wasn't such a good investment."

Gavin looked my way. "You're quite correct. We got caught up in the same financial meltdown that hit so many in this country. And we wound up on the hook for this enormous loan."

Mother tsk-tsked, then said, "That would certainly strain any relationship." (She has a sincere tsk-tsk and a fake tsk-tsk, and this was the latter.)

I asked Gavin, "What will happen now with the loan?"

He sighed. "There will be a payout on the insurance policy covering the home, to apply to the loan. After that, if there's anything left in the estate, with luck it might cover the balance due. Otherwise I'll have to take out a second mortgage on *this* place." Very quietly, he said, "Sarah isn't wild about that."

Mother asked, "Was there a will?"

He shrugged a shoulder. "I don't really know. If so, it could be in a safe deposit box somewhere, or might have been destroyed in the fire. Regardless, I expect the Historical Preservation Society to be the benefactor."

Mother shifted gears. "Had James ever mentioned the name Leon Jones?"

Gavin's brow tightened. ". . . No. I don't believe so. Who is he?"

"The janitor at the Playhouse," Mother said, adding, "He seems to have disappeared."

This time both shoulders shrugged. "Afraid I can't help you with that. . . . There's a Miguel Something from the Playhouse, who'd been doing some painting at the mansion . . . according to Evelyn Snydacker, anyway, who keeps me informed whether I want to be or not." He paused, his eyes narrowing. "Sheriff, who actually *did* die in the fire? Is that why you mentioned that janitor?"

Sarah materialized in the mouth of the living room, and announced, "We really should go, dear."

Meaning we should too.

"Just one more question, Mr. Sutter," Mother said. "Where were you between the hours of five o'clock on Monday and noon on Tuesday?"

Sarah looked sharply at Mother. "Don't tell me Gavin is a *suspect* now? Haven't we suffered enough indignities?"

Her husband raised a hand. "Now, darling, the sheriff is only doing her job." He cupped his chin with a hand. "Let's see. . . . I had dinner here with Sarah, then watched the Cardinals play the Brewers, and went to bed about eleven. The next morning I woke up at six forty-five, showered, dressed, had breakfast, and got to the plant by eight. I stayed there until one, when I left to have lunch with a coworker. Would you like his name?"

I think Gavin expected her to demur, but when Mother didn't, he told her who it was, and she wrote it down in the notepad.

Mother stood and so did I. "Thank you for your time, Mr. Sutter."

"Happy to help," he said, not sounding happy at all.

As we exited, I may have left behind a

small brown stain on the beige carpet by the couch where my feet had been planted, but I couldn't be sure. A DNA test would have led to Sushi, I'm afraid.

According to Mother, Evelyn Snydacker would be playing bridge this morning at the Serenity Country Club, as was her regular wont. Knowing how much Mother hated being interrupted during her own bridge games, I suggested she interview the woman later.

"Nonsense," Mother replied. "Evelyn will *relish* the intrusion when she finds out the sheriff wants to talk to her. She loves being the center of attention. You know the type!"

I take the Fifth.

The country club was located across what Mother and I refer to as the Treacherous By-pass, because the four-lane highway had few stoplights and no middle area for a driver to hole up at after a misjudged attempted crossing. Once again, we managed to survive, and I pulled in the country club's drive.

I found a spot for the C-Max in a lot full of BMWs, Audis, Cadillacs, and Lincolns, and we extracted ourselves from our puny but conscientious hybrid.

From the outside, the modern structure might be mistaken for a millionaire's home

— beautifully landscaped, with drive-up portico, and an outdoor pool (closed for the season) off to one side.

We went through double etched-glass doors into a vestibule, where a couple of facing faux Louis XV chairs stood guard, then crossed through another set of etched-glass doors, and entered an expansive greeting area where two floral couches were separated by a round cherrywood table topped with a large oriental vase filled with fresh fall flowers.

To the right, a carpeted hallway of geometric design led to the barroom, and banquet room beyond. The left-hand hallway accessed various offices. Downstairs was the clubhouse with a smaller, more casual eating venue.

An officious-looking gent approached from the office wing. I didn't recognize him, but Mother seemed to.

His expression was one of alarm, which could be due to Mother's official capacity as sheriff, or her personal capacity as troublemaker. Six of one.

"Greetings, Mr. Eggler," Mother said with a polite smile. "I need to speak with Evelyn Snydacker."

His alarm morphed into concern. "Oh, dear! I'm afraid she's in the middle of a game at the moment."

Mother's smile would have remained frozen on her face however long it took for Eggler to come to his senses.

He finally capitulated, saying, "I'll go get her."

"Thank you," Mother replied graciously. "You'll find us in the bar."

While he scurried off, we made our way along the hallway to a private room with windows facing the rolling golf course, a cozy fireplace (not in use), burgundy-colored leather chairs, small cherrywood accent tables, and of course a fully stocked bar, which was unattended at the moment. The entire room was unpopulated, unless you counted us.

Mother picked one of two comfy chairs in front of the fireplace, while I sat near the bar, wondering how I could get a soft drink. Was my ex-officio position enough to risk going around the bar and commandeering a Sprite?

Mrs. Snydacker appeared in a forest-green pants suit, her face cheeks flushed — or perhaps she was just overly rouged — and hurried toward Mother.

"Vivian!" she exclaimed. "How nice to see you."

Mother gestured for the woman to take

the other chair. "My apologies, my dear, to have taken you away from your game. I know how important that is."

Mother's sarcasm was hidden from Mrs. Snydacker but in clear view of her deputy daughter.

The bridge player, now having lit, replied, "That's quite all right, Vivian. . . . We have a roaming substitute. And besides, at the moment, I was the dummy."

Why don't you take that one?

The woman leaned toward Mother conspiratorially. "I heard you were in the hospital, Vivian. Do tell me all about it."

Inquiring minds want to know.

Mother said, "I'm not here to talk about myself, dear."

"Oh," Mrs. Snydacker said curtly, taking that as a rebuke. To be fair, a visit from Mother when she wasn't in the mood to talk about herself was fairly rare. "Then, what is it you want?"

"Just the facts," Mother said, knowing Mrs. Snydacker was a woman of a certain age who would understand the *Dragnet* reference. "When did you last have contact with James Sutton?"

She sat back, raised a forefinger to her suspiciously rosy cheek. "Well, let's see. . . . It would have been Monday evening when

Jimmy called me at home — to thank me for the new grant."

"Do you recall what time?"

"Around seven o'clock, I would say. I was washing up the dinner dishes."

"And how did James sound?"

"Well, *pleased,* naturally." Mrs. Snydacker frowned. "But I did have to give him a bit of bad news."

While Mother waited for the woman to explain, I left my chair and went behind the bar to see what I could confiscate. A pro bono ex-officio has certain rights.

The president of the Historical Preservation Society was saying, "I told James that after *this* grant, there would unfortunately be no more money available for the Wentworth mansion."

Mother straightened, eyes and nostrils flaring — she darn near whinnied. "As a member of the committee, why was *I* not party to this decision?"

Mrs. Snydacker made a scoffing sound. "Vivian, since you were elected sheriff, you haven't attended a single meeting."

"Perhaps I missed one."

"You were absent at the last three meetings."

"Well, I *have* been a little busy!" Mother replied, miffed.

I located the button for Sprite on the soft drink gun dispenser, pushed it, and began filling a glass, having already helped myself to ice.

"There's no point in discussing this," the woman said, miffed right back at her. "You would have been overruled, in any event. We were in unanimous agreement that no more grants would be given for what had increasingly become a money pit. Besides, why bother discussing it now? The point is moot, now that the mansion has gone up in smoke." She seemed to know her tone was getting snippy, and added in a somber tone, "Tragically."

Behind the bar, I also found some fruit in a little fridge and tossed a maraschino cherry and orange wedge into the glass. I looked around for a little paper umbrella, but no dice.

Mrs. Snydacker went on, "And now we can use our funds for other endeavors — projects that require but a single grant, such as repairing the swing bridge at the park or the marquee on the old Palace Theater."

Mother's shoulders sagged a little. "You're right, of course. But I did love that old place."

Mrs. Snydacker's tone turned sympathetic. "I know you did, Vivian. So did I. So did we all! But some things are beyond saving." What she said next seemed to be a thought better not spoken out loud. "In fact, some things are better off gone."

Mother snapped out of her funk. "I need to know your whereabouts from Monday evening through noon on Tuesday."

Mrs. Snydacker goggled at Mother.

"Now, don't bother looking offended, Evelyn. I have to ask everyone I interview that question. Strictly routine."

Dragnet again. And those two were old enough to remember Ben Alexander, not just Harry Morgan. (If you understand that reference without a Google search, you and Mother may have been classmates.)

Settled back down, Mrs. Snydacker nodded her understanding. "As I said, I was at home Monday night when I received James's call, and I didn't go out that evening at all. Tuesday morning, I dropped by to see you at the hospital around eight, had that interview with the *Serenity Sentinel* nine-ish, and got home about ten." She leaned toward Mother. "Is this about James being found in the woods? After the misidentification of whoever died in the fire? Surely you don't think I had anything to do with *any* of that!"

Mother responded with her most mysterious smile, rose, and said, "Thank you, Evelyn. I'm sure you'll be wanting to get back to your game."

Mrs. Snydacker stood. "You could have at least thrown me a crumb, Vivian."

"A crumb, dear?"

"Some morsel of information. Something to share!"

"Ah. Well. Certainly. The explosion came from a propane tank."

"Everybody already knows that!"

"How about this. . . . It was Sushi who sniffed out James's resting place."

Mrs. Snydacker goggled again. "Really! My word. That little darling canine *is* a marvel. Well, at least that's *something* to tell the ladies. Makes a rather cute anecdote, really."

Real cute. Dog smells corpse in the woods. Delightful.

After the woman left, I took her place.

Mother eyed my drink. "I don't suppose you could make me a hot toddy without the toddy."

"And what exactly would that be?"

"Hot water and honey, hold the whiskey."

"Didn't spot any honey back there, honey. Here, try some of this." I handed her my glass. "Not to worry. No booze to muddle your medication."

"Or yours, either."

"Or mine."

Mother in particular had learned not to mix alcohol with her medication, after once ending up in Poughkeepsie without knowing how she'd gotten there. Well, she sort of knew. A bus.

Mother took a sip of my drink, then plucked out the cherry, bit off the stem, and chewed the plump redness, her eyebrows knitting together.

"Something?" I asked.

She took a moment to chew and swallow, then replied. "Evelyn *does* have a motive for starting the fire, you know."

"I don't know. Give."

"She obviously has her own pet projects that took precedence in her bridge player's mind."

"What? Because of some grant money she could access? That's a little far-fetched." I reclaimed my drink and downed it. "Come on, Joe Friday — let's go."

Benjamin Wentworth lived downtown in the refurbished six-story Grand Hotel, which had been converted into luxury condos. On the drive, Mother told me that the heir of the Wentworth antiques had recently put his condo on the market, as he planned to relocate to Arizona where he was building a home with his new, much younger wife.

We took the elevator to the top, stepping off into beautifully carpeted luxury. Each floor had two condominiums, front and rear, and Mother rang the buzzer on the door of the former, which faced the river.

After waiting about thirty seconds, she tried again, and almost immediately the door opened, the white-haired distinguished Wentworth wearing a very uncustomary gray sweatshirt and jeans, along with a perplexed expression.

He asked, rather tightly, "Sheriff. Something I can do for you?"

"You may start with inviting me in," she replied.

I was invisible, merely an extension of her, not even garnering a glance from the man.

"Well, certainly," he said, backing out of the way.

We paused inside the marble-floored vestibule, as Wentworth closed the door, then moved around us, indicating we were to follow him down the corridor.

He took us to a spacious room where the living area was to the left and kitchen to the right. The furnishings were tasteful and expensive, the appliances top-of-the-line. But most impressive were the windows running the expanse of the front wall, offering a view of the Mississippi River, sparkling in the late morning sun, as if diamonds had been cast out upon the waters. He could afford it.

Mother, who had been appraising the open boxes resting on the Persian rug, cartons partially filled with leather-bound tomes from a nearby bookcase, asked, "Moving so soon?"

"Yes," Wentworth replied. "Jessica's been in Phoenix for several weeks now, supervising construction of our new home, and I'm anxious to join her. The moving company is coming next week."

Mother nodded. "Heading all the way to Arizona. That'll be quite an expense, I would imagine."

"Yes, but better than having to furnish from scratch, with what little I could get from a moving sale." Wentworth shrugged. "And I found an area company that was quite reasonable — Reliable Hauling?"

"Not familiar with them," Mother admitted.

Nor was I.

Since he had yet to offer her a seat, Mother took it upon herself to cross to a brocade couch, where she plopped down, leaving Wentworth with limited options — a

212

nearby armchair or just stand there. He chose the former.

Rather than join Mother, I went over to gaze out the windows, where along the riverfront a train was chugging discreetly by, the city having recently established the downtown a "whistle-free" zone. Before that, city center dwellers would peel themselves off their ceilings when the trains came blaring through in the middle of the night.

Mother was saying, "I assume you're aware of all the latest developments."

"Indeed," our host said, nodding. "I'm certainly pleased you weren't hurt, Vivian. And I do hope you find James's killer, and whoever it was who got himself caught in the fire." He paused. "But I don't know what any of that has to do with me."

Wentworth seemed on the defensive, as if Gavin or Evelyn had tipped him off that Mother might come around. He appeared ready with his answers.

No, he hadn't seen or talked to James Sutter in quite some time. No, he hadn't left the condo Monday evening through Tuesday noon, busy packing as he was.

Mother, her professional demeanor turning conciliatory, said, "You're going to be missed, Benjamin. Won't seem right around the old town without you. The Wentworths

213

had a lot to do with the success of Serenity through the years." She sighed. "But, I suppose I can understand that there's nothing left to keep you here, now that the mansion is gone. I do hope you're not too upset about the loss of the contents."

"Upset?" He smiled just a little. "To be brutally honest, no. Those antiques had become a collective albatross around my neck." He raised a hand. "Don't misunderstand. I don't take it lightly that a life was lost in that fire. And as for whatever happened to James, and how it might relate to all this . . . very distressing."

He didn't seem very distressed to me.

"But," he was saying, "I'm free now from the shackles of my great-grandfather's will, and will no longer have to pay the exorbitant insurance premiums on material items for which I have no sentimental feelings whatsoever, and — actually, frankly — came to loathe."

But he wouldn't loathe the huge insurance payout those "material items" would generate.

If Mother seemed surprised by his frank admission, she didn't betray it a whit.

"I quite understand, Benjamin," she said. "It might be different, had you grown up around those antiques, living with them, utilizing them. I've always felt one must have an emotional attachment through fond memories of a physical object in order to truly care about it."

I turned from the window. "We have people coming into our shop all the time," I said, "who ooooh and ahhhhh over the darndest things, just because they used to have one like it."

Both Wentworth and Mother were looking at me as if they hadn't previously noticed my presence. The sheriff shot an unappreciative glance my way. "Yes, thank you, dear. . . . Benjamin, when will you be leaving town?"

"The middle of next week," he said. "I dislike being away from my bride for any extended time."

"Going so soon?" Mother asked. "Isn't it necessary that you wait until you've settled with the insurance company?"

He waved that off with a parchment-skinned hand. "That can be handled long-distance, and through my lawyer, if need be." Our host stood and performed an excuse for a smile. "But, until then, I'm at your disposal, Vivian . . . Sheriff. And you can always reach me on my cell. You do have that number?"

"I do," Mother said, but she hadn't

budged from her seat on the sofa. "One more thing, if it's not too much trouble — in regard to the Tiffany lava vase that always graced the table in the mansion's entryway."

Why was she showing him her hole card on such an early round?

"What about it?" he asked. With a just a hint of impatience.

"It would seem," she said, "that a vase looking exactly like it showed up for sale on the internet, just a day after the fire."

Wentworth frowned. "What are you saying?"

"From where I sit" — and she *was* still sitting — "that strikes me as quite a coincidence. Wouldn't you agree?"

She was watching him closely, studying him as he took a moment to gather his thoughts before responding.

Finally he said, "Not necessarily. I believe Tiffany made quite a few vases in his volcanic series, vases that looked nearly identical, even handcrafted as they were."

Mother smiled. "A reasonable-enough explanation. Still, it might be worth checking into."

And now, at last, she stood.

"Come, Brandy," she said, as if about to toss me a biscuit. "And thank you, Benjamin, for your time — we can find our way out."

From the condominiums it was just a stone's throw to Cliff Reed's office on the third floor of the First National Bank, so we left the car in the lot and hoofed it on over.

In the outer office, the strawberry blonde receptionist informed us that Cliff had a customer at the moment.

That didn't suit Mother.

Standing tall before the desk, she said, "Please inform Mr. Reed that the sheriff is here and, while I certainly understand that he has business to conduct as an insurance agent, the sheriff, as a duly elected representative of justice, has a murder investigation to carry out."

The receptionist squinted at Mother, trying to bring her into focus. "And you're the sheriff, right?"

"I am indeed. They do not give this uniform to just anybody."

"I'm not surprised. I never saw one like that before. Please take a seat."

We did, while the receptionist used the phone to inform her boss of his visitors.

Mother shot me a glare. "What are you smiling about?"

"Nothing."

We had barely settled into our chairs when

a plump woman well known to us, Mrs. Fusselman, emerged from the hallway, dragging her coat while stuffing some papers into a large tote. It appeared she'd just been rather rudely ejected from Cliff's office. The lady gave Mother a peeved look as she trundled toward the door.

The receptionist's intercom buzzed, and Cliff's voice could be heard saying to send Mother back.

We found Cliff Reed behind his desk, with work spread out in front of him like an unappetizing banquet, and he did not rise when we entered.

Still, he said warmly, "Hello, Vivian . . . Sheriff. Brandy, nice to see you again."

While I hung back, Mother moved to the visitor's chair opposite the agent. Suddenly obsequious, she said, "I *do* hope I didn't cause you any distress with Mrs. Fusselman. I would have been *more than happy* to wait."

Ha.

"No, not at all," Cliff assured her. "As a matter of fact, I'm glad you came when you did." He chuckled a little. "The old gal does love to gossip, and we'd finished with our business."

"These gossips," Mother said, shaking her head, smiling.

These gossips.

"Now," Cliff said, "what can I do for you?"

No specific queries about finding James, the explosion, or the mystery man in the fire. Interesting.

Mother, all business now, said, "I'm here to inquire about the insurance policies taken out by James Sutter and Benjamin Wentworth."

"You're here in your official capacity?"

"But of course. I made that clear to your receptionist."

He sat back, tented his fingers. His eyebrows went up. "I thought perhaps you might be representing the Historical Preservation Society. There'll be no payout on the mansion itself, I'm afraid."

Mother leaned forward. "Surely the structure was insured. The bank would have required that for the mortgage!"

"It was, and they did."

"Then why no payout?"

"Because . . ." Cliff took in air, let it out. "James allowed the policy to lapse, two months ago."

"Good Lord," Mother exclaimed. "And you didn't *know* about it?"

The insurance agent sat forward, elbows on the desk. "Not until the company holding the policy notified me that the premium was overdue. Which is why I paid him a visit."

"And?"

"And . . . James said the check must have been lost or delayed in the mail, and he said he would immediately put a stop payment on it, then send the company another. But, apparently, he never did."

I asked, "Is that why Gavin looked so upset when he came to see you on Wednesday?"

Cliff looked at me, as if I'd tossed cold water in his face. "What?"

"I saw him when I was leaving your office."

Nervous smile. "Ah . . . yes. That was indeed the reason."

Who says *indeed* anymore?

Mother said, "Quite understandable, since he had indeed cosigned the mortgage loan."

Oh. Never mind.

She went on: "I hope he didn't blame *you* for the snafu."

She never could resist a dig.

"I don't believe he did," Cliff muttered.

"Hopefully," she said, "Benjamin will have better luck with *his* insurance coverage. Do you expect any problems with the settlement on the antiques? I assume I can ask that simple question without a court order."

Cliff swallowed, then shook his head. "No. The required appraisals are in order. And, as soon as the insurance company has done its investigation, and state and local fire marshals have completed theirs — which should be any time now — Mr. Wentworth will receive full coverage of the policy. I can assure you that."

"Of course," Mother commented, "it helps to have a tenacious and smart agent in one's corner to move things along."

"Naturally, insurance companies like to drag things out, so, yes, it *does* help to have someone like me pushing them."

"For a consideration from the insured?" she asked sweetly.

"Consideration?"

"Kickback, then."

His smile disappeared. "Sheriff, because you're new on the job, I'm going to forget that you said that."

Unfazed, Mother produced her notepad and pen. "Just a few questions. When was the last time you spoke to James?"

"Last week, when I went to see him about the lapsed policy. As I said."

"And what were your movements from Monday night through noon on Tuesday?"

Cliff swiveled in his chair, thinking. "Let's see . . . I was at home Monday night, and came to work Tuesday morning at eight and saw clients all morning. My receptionist can corroborate that."

"Can anyone vouch for you on Monday night?"

He looked down at some papers on the desk, as if they might have the answer. "No. I was alone at home. My wife and I have recently separated."

"I'm sorry to hear that, Mr. Reed. I do hope you both can work things out."

He nodded.

Mother returned the notepad to her pocket. "Thank you for your time."

He nodded again, managed a smile.

We left.

Walking back to the C-Max, I said, "You've got a real doozy of a problem, haven't you?"

"I have any number of doozies going in my life, dear, at any given time. Please quantify your remark."

I shrugged. "It's what Evelyn let slip . . . that some things are better off gone. Those four people you just interviewed? They *all* seem to benefit from that fire, or thought they would."

"True," Mother said. "To varying degrees, but . . . true."

We had arrived at the car.

"So maybe you shouldn't be looking for a single killer," I said. "But several."

"Or all of them," Mother commented. "As in one big, fat doozy of a conspiracy."

A TRASH 'N' TREASURES TIP

When selling antiques online through an auction site, make sure you are allowed to set a reserve price. That way, the item will not be sold for anything below that price. Mother has been so confident at times that she didn't bother with requesting a reserve. That's how she came to sell a silver tea set for $2.98.

CHAPTER NINE:
IN WHICH VIVIAN PLAYS IT BY EAR AND BRANDY GETS HER NOSE OUT OF JOINT

My darlings, when last you left us, Brandy and I were about to get into our C-Max after my interrogation of Cliff Reed (actually, law enforcement prefers the term *interview* to *interrogation* these days, but I don't have to play their reindeer games). Just then my cell phone rang. Well, actually sang — the "I Fought the Law" cover by the Bobby Fuller Four — with the little I.D. window identifying Jake as the caller.

Even though this was an inopportune time to talk with my grandson, with Brandy in close proximity and unaware of Jake's Chicagoland involvement in the current case, I could not resist talking to the lad. I was just too anxious to find out what he learned on his adventure.

Just to be clear, gentle reader, you have heard/read Jake's end of our conversation in his chapter, earlier in this book, and didn't he do a nice job! Storytelling must be in the Borne DNA, don't you think?

I stepped away from the car (and my mistrustful daughter) to take the call, making sure not to give away whom I was talking to, pleased as punch by Jake's report, and how well he had done. (Do you know what flashed through my mind? The ending of the movie *Auntie Mame,* when Mame — so brilliantly brought to life by Rosalind Russell — was leading her grandson up the grand staircase, painting a picture in the air of the wonderful adventures they would have together now that her son/his father was too old for such things.)

But perhaps because of the length of the conversation and my giggling toward the end of the discussion, Brandy got suspicious and, after I'd signed off, inquired about the call.

"Oh, that was Jake," I said casually, slipping my cell back into a pocket. "He was home with a little tummy ache today. I'm sure he'll call you later. No worries."

She had her hands on her hips. "Uh-huh. Get into the car. Unless you'd like to have this little chat out here."

Sensing she had ascertained my deception, I preferred not having a chat with her at all. But I chose the privacy of the C-Max over a public display.

When Brandy was behind the wheel, and I was in the passenger seat — perhaps I should say hot seat — she stared at me with unblinking accusatory eyes.

She asked in a voice as flat as if a steamroller had traveled over her words, "Did you ask Jake to skip school and go to a downtown Chicago antiques store to check out that vase?"

I gave her my most winning smile. "Yes, dear. I'd been meaning to tell you about that, but it slipped my mind. And he did a simply *splendid* job! He discovered the name of the man who sold it to the store, and even followed him to where he worked."

She trembled.

She reddened.

She raged.

"*Mother!* How could you put Jake in danger, *again*? That man he followed could be the killer! How could you do that to my son — your *grandson*? And what if Roger found out? He'd make sure Jake would never have any further contact with you — and who could blame him? And maybe he would banish *me* for allowing you to do it!"

"Exactly why I protected you, dear, and handled it without involving you."

"You expect my ex to *buy* that? You've put

all of us in jeopardy!"

The poor girl was sputtering now. So sad to see an intelligent person lose control.

"Brandy," I said calmly, "firstly, Jake was very careful not to use his real name, and covered his tracks in a manner that would not lead anyone to the Naperville home. Secondly, he had more success in getting information than many a seasoned investigator would have, and you really should be proud."

"That's supposed to make me feel better?"

"Dear, he's fourteen," I said, "not a baby. He's really growing up, our Jake."

"He's a minor, Mother! And when you ask him to do something, of course he will — he loves you, and wants to please you." She paused, adding, as if to herself, "And I think he likes playing detective a little too much, too. But it's not play, Mother, it's real, dangerous life!" She waggled a finger. "You have to *promise* me you won't involve Jake *ever* again."

"Very well. I promise."

"Were your fingers crossed?"

"No."

But my hammer toes were.

Brandy sighed. She seemed to still be trembling somewhat.

"All right then," she said. "We won't talk anymore about this." She started the engine. "Where would the sheriff like to be taken now?"

I had the girl drop me off at the county jail, where I checked in at the office. Deputy Chen was out dealing with a domestic dispute, so I sat at my desk and logged in my movements for the day.

Then I used several law enforcement databases on my computer to look for anything on an Alek Wozniack (thank you, Jake!), turning up some interesting information.

I called Chief Cassato.

"We need to talk," I said, "but not on the phone."

"Can it wait until tomorrow?"

"No. Meet me at Cinders at six."

A long pause. "Why there?"

"Because that's where I'm going to be," I said, and ended the call.

At five, I left the jail and walked over to Main Street to a certain bar where my new informant could usually be found at this hour, in the company of a special friend.

Now, I know what longtime readers are thinking: *Wait a minute, why aren't you going to your usual haunt, Hunter's Hardware? That unique establishment with the bar in back,*

*where customers could drink and then buy
electrical tools and go home to use them and
maybe hurt themselves . . . and encounter the
owner, Mary, who lost a leg on the* Jaws *ride
at Universal Studios, who put a gag order on
you not to mention the accident anymore . . .
and her husband, Junior, the bartender who
liked his own wares too much and was no help
at all with your inquiries . . . and your informant, Henry, the old doctor-cum-barfly who
ended his career by removing a patient's
gallbladder instead of the scheduled ap-
pendectomy?*

Granted, your thoughts may have been
more succinct.

Well, I'll *tell* you what happened! Mary
and Junior sold their hardware store and
the new owner turned the back bar into a
coffee shop, and Henry left for Chattanooga
to live with a relative dedicated to drying
him out once and for all. I know. I shall miss
them, too.

But one door closes and another one
opens. And this new door took me into the
most unusual gin mill in town, located on
the first floor of another boxcar-style Victorian brick building in the business district,
an establishment I didn't even know existed
until Brandy brought me here one evening
when I was at a low ebb (because of the

loss of Hunter's). That was where, and when, she introduced me to Nona and Nona's unusual friend Zelda. (Actually both Nona and Zelda were/are unusual.)

But first a word (actually a number of words) about Renny, the owner of Cinders, a unique lady in her early fifties with a bubbly personality, long blond hair, pretty features, curvaceous figure, and a preference for leopard-print attire.

Renny is an enthusiastic buyer of oddball collectibles, filling her drinking emporium with hundreds of pop-culture castaways, all available for sale, although nothing is marked. If you see something you want, make an offer — Renny may or may not accept said offer, depending upon her whim and current cash flow.

It wasn't unusual for a customer who'd gotten a little tipsy to be seen leaving with a life-size standee of Mr. Spock tucked under an arm and a *Star Wars* lightsaber in hand, or admiring that tushy-extended poster of Farrah Fawcett on a skateboard.

Without knowing it, or perhaps sensing a coming trend, Renny had, in her years of largely indiscriminate collecting, made the bar a magnet for the local hipster crowd — twenty- and thirty-somethings and assorted oddballs just loved to hang out there.

Inside the entrance on the left was a huge completely furnished dollhouse, as well as a vast collection of Elvis memorabilia. Continuing along the left-hand wall was a long bar with a dozen red vinyl bucket-seat chairs, a row of lava lamps providing ambience.

Hugging the right wall, and nearly as long as the bar, was a hand shuffleboard game with little tables and chairs to one side for players to keep score. Following this came a 1950s jukebox, then a rather impressive collection of Marilyn Monroe and Betty Boop collectibles, all basking in the glow of hundreds upon hundreds of twinkle lights of varied colors strung everywhere.

And that is but a sample of the first of four rooms.

Renny, behind the bar, smiled upon seeing me. "Hello, Vivian. Your usual?"

This bartender never had to ask if I was off-duty, being well aware that my preferred drink was a Shirley Temple.

"Yes, thank you," I replied, approaching the bar.

Nona was seated at the very end, a glass of white wine before her; the chair next to her was vacant, an empty tumbler on the counter. Otherwise no other customer occupied this room.

I walked over to Nona, a slender woman in her mid-twenties with a narrow face, thin lips, long dark hair, and large purple-framed glasses. She wore an oversize brown leather bomber jacket, a short red-and-tan plaid skirt, ripped black tights, and floral combat boots. When I was a child, one might have called Nona a beatnik.

I asked, "And how are you doing this fine day, my dear?"

"Hunky-dory," she said.

I nodded to the empty chair. "And Zelda? How is she faring?"

Nona shrugged. "You can ask her yourself when she comes back from the ladies'."

"Might she like another drink?" I offered.

"I believe she would," Nona responded.

I turned my neck to look up the line. "Renny, one more of whatever Zelda is having."

"Sure thing," the owner replied.

I took the red bucket seat next to Zelda's and waited silently, seeing no need to converse further until she — my new informant — had returned. Nona was rather tight-lipped, you see. Zelda was the Chatty Cathy of the duo.

Renny delivered my Shirley Temple (with extra cherries) along with a tumbler of whiskey on the rocks, placed them on the

232

counter, and moved off to other duties.

Suddenly, Nona said, "She's back."

I addressed the vacant chair between us. "And how is Zelda this fine evening?"

You see, dear reader, Zelda exists only in the imagination of Nona, who is a tulpamancer, or "tulpa" for short. Tulpamancy is a mental condition in which a person will summon an imaginary companion, not unlike a child who may go through an invisible friend phase. For tulpas, however, the attachments do not disappear with age, but only grow stronger.

Little is known about tulpamancy — it might indeed be a form of mental illness, although some see it as a manifestation of the paranormal. But as a whole, these imaginary friends have a positive influence, and the voices that tulpas hear in their heads from these attachments are nothing like the ones who talk to me when I go off my bipolar medication. Those babies can be bad influences!

I continued talking to the chair. "Zelda, you might be of some help to me in my capacity as sheriff. Would you mind if I ask you a few questions?"

About ten seconds passed.

Then Nona spoke, "She says that's cool with her. And she's glad you weren't hurt when the propane tank blew up."

Apparently Zelda read the *Serenity Sentinel.* "You're too kind, Zelda."

I took a sip of my drink — Renny always mixed just the right combination of grenadine syrup and ginger ale — and collected my thoughts; my questions to Zelda needed to be concise, since her answers had to be relayed through the more taciturn Nona.

A pity Zelda and I couldn't converse directly!

"Zelda, would you happen to know Leon Jones?" I asked. "He's a janitor employed at the Playhouse."

After a moment, Nona said, "Yes, she does."

"Is he involved in selling drugs?"

Another ten seconds. "She says Leon is a source for obtaining marijuana but not a big dealer. Mostly, he sells from his own stash when he needs cash."

"Nona, inquire if you would if Zelda might know anything else about him."

"Sheriff," Nona said, mildly exasperated, "she's sitting right there! Please direct your questions to *her.* Don't be rude. She *can* hear you."

"Oh. My apologies." I repeated my query to the chair.

Nona listened to Zelda, then said, "She's

heard that Leon's left town. But that's all she knows about that."

I addressed my next inquiry to both women. "I understand that you two rent the upper floor of a house down the block from the Wentworth mansion."

Nona nodded. Not sure about Zelda.

I followed up: "Has there been any excess activity going on around there recently?"

Nona asked, "Like maybe Mr. Sutter was dealing in drugs, you mean?"

As unlikely as that seemed, I confirmed the query with a nod.

Nona consulted with Zelda. "Not really. At least no one looking suspicious had been hanging around there." She leaned toward the empty chair, bent her head, listened, then straightened. "Zelda wants to know if it was James who was found in the woods. And was it somebody else who died at the mansion."

"Zelda is correct. We don't know who that body belonged to."

Nona said, "Just a minute . . . Zelda wants to tell you something about that night."

For an endless thirty seconds I waited with bated breath. You know, really it should be baited breath, don't you think? Anyway, I waited.

Then Nona said, "Mr. Sutter received two

visitors that evening. Zelda doesn't know their names, but one was that lady who runs the Historical Preservation Society, and the other was a tall man with short dark-blond hair, about forty, who Zelda thinks might be a relative of that Sutter guy."

Evelyn and Gavin. Interesting!

"This is important, Zelda," I said to the chair. "Did they come together, or separately? And at what time? Also, what was their demeanor? Normal? Angry? What was your impression?"

A full minute passed. I resisted shaking the chair to get her to talk.

Finally Nona said, "Zelda says they came separately. The woman first, at about eight o'clock. The man later, maybe nine or nine-thirty. They each stayed about fifteen or twenty minutes. The lady seemed upset when she came out, and the man looked mad when he left."

I was digesting that information when the door opened and Tony strode in. As usual in work mode, he wore a tan trench coat flung over his usual light blue shirt, navy striped tie, gray slacks, and brown shoes.

By the chief's befuddled expression as he took in his surroundings, I was able to deduce he'd never been inside Cinders before.

236

He spotted me and walked over.

"Chief Cassato," I said. "I'd like you to meet Nona."

He nodded at the woman. "Nona," he said.

"And this," I went on, gesturing to the empty chair, "is Zelda. Say hello."

Tony looked at the chair. Tony's mouth dropped open. Finally a word came out of it: "Hello."

A few moments later, Nona said, "She says 'hi' to you, too, Chief. She says she's a fan."

". . . Thank you?" Tony, barely hiding his impatience, said to me, "Ah, Vivian — you wanted to talk to me?"

I downed the rest of my Shirley Temple.

"In the back," I said, and slid out of the bucket chair.

As he walked with me, he said, "What was *that* about?"

"Are you familiar with the movie *Harvey*? That wonderful, whimsical Jimmy Stewart vehicle?"

He frowned. "That invisible white rabbit thing?"

"That's right. While Zelda *is* invisible, she isn't a pooka. The pooka, like Harvey the big white rabbit, appears here and there, now and then, to this one and that one.

We're talking *tulpa* here."

"So Zelda's not a pooka. She's a tulpa."

I shook my head. "No, it's *Nona* who's the tulpa. Do try to keep up. *Zelda* is my new informant."

Tony said, "Your new informant is an invisible woman."

But then so many women in our society are invisible, aren't they? I decided not to share this pithy observation with the police chief. I mean, he wasn't even ready for a tulpa yet, was he?

"That's right, Chief." So difficult to stop calling him "Chiefie," but then as sheriff I did need to maintain a certain decorum. "Do you find the notion of an invisible informant surprising?"

"Vivian," the chief said, massaging his forehead with the fingertips of his left hand, "nothing you say or do anymore surprises me."

"Headache, dear? Tough day?"

"About average if long," he said slowly. "This headache just came on all of a sudden."

We had paused before a beaded-curtained doorway.

"I always travel with pain medication," I said. "What do you want? Aspirin, ibuprofen, acetaminophen, naproxen . . ."

"Do you have any Tylenol in a tampered-with bottle?"

"Oh, Chiefie, you're a card! Sorry. That was a slip."

He sighed. "Where are we headed? How far back does this thing go?"

"This way. Making progress!"

We went through the beads into the next room, which contained an assortment of vintage arcade games — Pac-Man, Donkey Kong, and Super Mario Bros. The walls were plastered with 1980s movies posters — *The Empire Strikes Back, Ghostbusters,* and *Ferris Bueller's Day Off* (Jake's favorite movie to watch when he's home sick).

A bamboo-strung archway took us into a third room, this one with a Mexican theme — tuck-and-roll upholstered car bench seats, Day of the Dead figurines, and colorful sombreros and serapes.

I parted red velvet curtains and we entered the last room, which was rather small and intimate, with only two options for sitting: a small couch in the shape of red lips, and a chair fashioned as a large black high-heeled shoe. The remainder of the space was taken up by fake palm trees whose branches were filled with an assortment of stuffed monkeys.

Tony looked at me, eyebrows raised.

"Really? Whatever happened to good old-fashioned deserted underground parking lots?"

"I thought we'd be more comfortable here," I said, and gestured to the seating. "Take your pick."

Tony took on the lower lip, apropos as he himself had a pouting lower lip at present, while I perched on the toe of the stiletto.

Waving his arms a bit, he said, "Vivian, what the hell is this about?"

An orange orangutan he'd knocked loose fell onto him, and he tossed it back up into the tree, where it didn't stay, so he sighed and just sat there with it on his lap.

I said, "Chief, I'm beginning to suspect a conspiracy between a number of people who may benefit from the mansion fire."

Tony frowned. "Any proof?"

"None at the moment — as Nero Wolfe says, 'It's merely conjecture.' But you know how right he always was!"

The chief was studying me much as I had studied Zelda's chair. "You came to this conclusion from your interviews today?"

"Yes. With Gavin Sutter, Evelyn Snydacker, Benjamin Wentworth, and Cliff Reed."

"Fill me in," he said.

"Okay, but we should start at the begin-

240

ning. And this begins with the vase."

"What vase?"

"The Tiffany lava vase that was always in the entryway of the Wentworth mansion . . . only when I entered that hell-fire inferno, it no longer was!"

". . . I think I *will* have some aspirin."

"Plain? Or ibuprofen, acetaminophen, or —"

"Anything!"

I located my zipper pocket pharmacy in my jumpsuit and handed him two naproxens. He popped them into his mouth and swallowed.

"I couldn't do that without water," I marveled.

"Vivian? I've had a long day. So, please, please . . . keep it simple."

"I will give it my very best shot." I took a deep breath. "When I went to see James the day of the fire, the vase was on the table in the entryway, but when I ran into the burning mansion that night it was gone. A vase just like it showed up on the internet for sale at a store in Chicago, and I had someone check it out. It was sold to the store by an individual named Alek Wozniak, who just happened to have served his sentence for robbery in the same prison at the same time as Leon Jones, the one-time janitor of the

Playhouse, who has since apparently absconded."

Tony was looking at me intently. "That was really very good, Vivian. Why can't you do that all the time?"

"Do what?"

He petted the monkey absently. "Never mind. Do you think Leon was involved?"

"Maybe. He could have been helping Miguel with the painting job at the mansion and gone back that evening, helped himself to the vase, and planned on fencing it through his old prison cohort."

The chief was nodding. "And then got surprised by James, and killed him, and set the fire for a cover-up. But that doesn't explain the other dead body." He paused. "What's the vase worth, anyway?"

"Eighty thousand," I said, "give or take a thousand or ten. At auction? *More.* So, fencing it . . . half of that estimate? And, maybe other things were taken. Possibly by other people involved in raiding the place of more precious, valuable antiques."

Tony was nodding. "Hard to determine in the fire, even with top investigators, what exactly was destroyed."

"Did you question Miguel today?"

"This morning, at the Playhouse. I accompanied forensics, who were looking for something that might have Leon's DNA."

"Any luck?" I asked.

Another nod. "An electric shaver in his locker — should get something from that."

"Any information yet on Leon's medical or dental records from the prison?"

"Requested but not yet received, although with the corpse in ashes, I don't see how that helps."

"True," I said. "But that information may come in handy. I'm inclined to think, however, that our mystery man is a transient from the homeless shelter."

He was nodding. "I did follow up on that. Someone who fits the profile was there for about a week before the fire, then left suddenly . . . which of course is not unusual. Folks move on in that realm without giving notice. We're trying to track the man to other area shelters."

Now I was nodding. "What about your interview with Miguel?"

Tony shrugged a shoulder. "He was co-operative. Claimed he worked at the mansion the day of the fire but knocked off around three in the afternoon."

"That was before I arrived. And his whereabouts that night?"

"Alone in his apartment. The next morning he stopped by the hospital to see you before going to work at the Playhouse."

My cell phone sang.

"Sheriff," Deputy Chen said excitedly. "Got a call from night security out at the gravel factory who says there's a truck submerged in one of their flooded pits."

"I'm on my way," I said.

I relayed the message to Tony.

"Even though this is on my patch," I said, "you are welcome to tag along."

He gave me a wry half smile.

Since I was without a vehicle, Tony drove us in his unmarked car, heading south to an area the locals call the Island, which it once had been way back when the town was founded, long before the Mighty Mississippi decided to reroute its course.

The Island's sandy soil was perfect for growing produce — especially melons, water and musk — which made something of a name for Serenity throughout the country for having the best such produce anywhere. The Island was also rich in other land resources, and the Serenity Sand and Gravel Company is where we were heading, just as the sun was setting.

In a few minutes, night would be closing in — not an ideal condition for conducting a search and rescue operation. But I had already jumped to the conclusion that this

would be a process of search, not rescue —
the truck had likely been there a few days,
ditched by Leon, who'd made other arrangements to disappear.

Tony turned off the main four-lane highway onto a two-lane, and after a few miles
took another turn toward the river, where
we rumbled along a dusty gravel road, then
finally passed through the open gates of the
Serenity Sand and Gravel Company, awash
in outside flood lights.

The chief pulled up to the office building,
a low-slung industrial affair with white
aluminum siding and a sloping roof, attached to a large tall structure. Long metal
conveyor belts led into the structure, used
for transporting large chunks of rock dug
from the earth, chiefly sandstone and limestone, up and inside to be crushed. Nearby,
waiting for the pulverized results, were a
number of truck loaders, as well as dump
trucks to transport the gravel to buyers.

As we got out of the car, a burly man
exited the office. He was wearing navy
slacks and a navy coat, zipped up, with the
name of a local security company on the
breast pocket.

After a quick introduction — his name
was Norman — I asked, "Well?"

"I was walking the grounds outside," he

said, "when I noticed the headlights of two cars in the distance, driving along a lane leading to one of the abandoned gravel pits. Not particularly unusual — kids go down there every once in a while, find the chain-link fence locked, turn around, and go some other place to party."

Before they were closed off, these gravel pits had been a favorite swimming destination for teens, the close proximity of the river filling the pits with water. But, tragically, too often kids drowned, due to ill-advised alcohol consumption and/or the tall weeds that grew on the bottom, prone to ensnaring legs.

"What time was this?" I asked.

"About half an hour ago," Norman said. "I watched from here for a while — maybe ten minutes — before taking the trouble to go out there, and sure enough, I saw lights going back along the lane." He paused. "Only it was just *one* set of lights."

"Go on," Tony said.

"So I head there, and could see that the chain on the fence gate had been cut, and I go through, but there's no vehicle. I shine my Maglite into the pit, and under the water, I can see the back end of a truck. Red. Like blood."

"Take us," I said, my supposition that the

truck had been ditched days before dissipating.

Tony turned to me. "Let's use Norman's vehicle to minimize the tracks."

We did.

While waiting for Serenity Search and Rescue to arrive (the tow truck would come along later), Tony and I scoured the immediate area with our flashlights, looking for other tire tracks or footprints or any evidence to preserve.

I spotted tire tracks that indicated one trespassing vehicle had pulled off to the side of the lane, in front of the fence gate, while another had continued on through, ending at the edge of the pit. Both sets appeared detailed enough that forensics might be able to make casts.

The two-man Search and Rescue team — Adam and Mark — arrived in their specially equipped van, and I indicated with a wave where they should park to avoid disrupting the evidence.

They got out, Adam wearing a diving suit and carrying a compact oxygen tank, and Mark hauling a duffel bag of tools. Both men were under forty and fit.

Our brief greetings took place at the edge of the pit.

"Anyone inside?" Adam asked.

"Unknown, but unlikely," I responded, shining my flashlight on the water's surface.

"Then I'll find the best place to hook the cable," Adam said.

"ETA of the tow truck?" Tony asked.

Mark said, "Maybe fifteen minutes."

While Adam put on his oxygen backpack, Mark unzipped the duffel bag and took out an underwater light that his partner would need.

Adam walked in his flippers to the edge of the pit, eased himself into the water, and disappeared beneath the surface.

Perhaps thirty seconds had passed when the diver's head reemerged, and he yanked out his mouthpiece.

"Get me the puncher!" he shouted to his partner.

The chief and I looked at each other; the spring-loaded tool was used for breaking a car's window, which meant that someone was indeed inside the cab.

And that someone must be Leon Jones, who did not perish in the fire after all but here, in a lonely gravel pit.

I said to Tony, "Looks like those prison records will come in handy after all."

Another minute crawled by while we waited above.

Then Adam reappeared, clutching a limp

body. As he began hauling it to the pit's edge, Mark jumped in to help, and together they eased the victim up and onto the ground, placing it on its back where it rested, too late to be revived, even though Mark tried.

I gathered that Tony was as dumbstruck as I.

"This *is* unfortunate," he said.

"It really is," I agreed. "Looks like I'm going to need a new stage manager."

MOTHER'S
TRASH 'N' TREASURES TIP

Sellers often overlook using social media as a way of attracting buyers. Post a picture of what you wish to sell on Facebook, Twitter, and Pinterest, and let your friends help spread the word. I've also found that having adorable Sushi in the photo, as well, increases interest. But it's also attracted unwanted offers from dog lovers wanting to buy the lovable furball.

Chapter Ten:
In Which Vivian Takes Center Stage and Brandy Waits for Her Cue

Nearing midnight, I started getting worried that Mother wasn't home yet. I'd sent her a text an hour ago, but she'd ignored it, and I was about to call her cell, when the front door opened.

"You look beat!" I said, concerned, as she almost staggered in. "Where have you been? What have you been up to?"

She climbed out of her sheriff's jacket, hung it up on the hook rack in the entry, then turned to me, her eyes lidded. "Tea, dear. Constant Comment."

I raised an eyebrow. "Has caffeine."

"Nothing will keep me awake tonight," she sighed wearily.

I frowned. "Spill. What's been going on?"

She gestured vaguely. "The tea, dear. And one of those biscotti biscuits."

Too eager for information to honor the niceties, I skipped the kettle and put a cup of water in the microwave.

When I returned to the living room, Mother was stretched out on the Victorian couch, sans shoes, a pillow beneath her head. She elbowed to a sitting position, and I handed her the cup on a saucer with the cookie tucked alongside.

I sat next to her, curling my legs beneath me.

Propped now, Mother took a sip, then said, "Miguel Ricardo was murdered tonight."

I stared at her in disbelief. "What does this mean?"

She went on to explain that her longtime Playhouse rival been found inside Leon Jones's truck, which had been submerged by parties unknown in one of the old water-filled gravel pits on the Island.

I asked, "Do we know who did it?"

She took a bite of the cookie, chewed, swallowed, but didn't answer.

"Oh, no," I said. "Not Alek Wozniak!"

"A possibility. Miguel might have been his connection to the vase, through Leon Jones." She paused. "And Wozniak would have had time to drive here after Jake saw him to then meet with Miguel."

I unfurled my legs. "Mother, if that's true, Jake can't know about it. He can't *ever* find out that his actions — directed by *you* —

may have caused Miguel's death!"

Mother said contritely, "I realize that."

"Do you?" I demanded, feeling sick to my stomach. "Is Jake in danger?"

"I don't believe so."

"But you can't be *sure,* can you? You can't be sure that Wozniak won't go after him!"

Mother put a hand on my knee. "Brandy, both Tony and I have been in touch with the Chicago PD — they know we want Wozniak for questioning in a murder inquiry, and they'll pick him up. They may have already." She went on, "In the meantime, I've called in a marker from an old friend who has, shall we say, associates in Chicago who will watch Jake's house until further notice. And our precious young man's every movement will be monitored until this thing is resolved."

Old friend? Associates?

I asked, "Do I want to know who your old friend is?"

"Best not."

But I could guess. A year ago Mother and I had traveled to the Big Apple to sell a rare Superman original drawing at a comic book convention (*Antiques Con*), and while there, she did a favor for a certain individual who some might refer to as a godfather, and not the kind who comes to the baptism.

Mother was saying, "Rest assured that Jake's welfare is well in hand. Now, why don't you go on up to bed?"

I didn't know whether to be distressed, furious, or relieved. "If anything happens to Jake —"

"It won't, dear. Get some sleep."

With a sigh that started at my toes, I went up to bed and curled up with Sushi, but sleep didn't come.

What could I do? Call Jake's father and say that Mother had again gotten Jake involved in a murder investigation, and our son might be in danger from the killer, but don't worry, because Mother has called in her mob contacts? *You* try to go to sleep in that situation.

But Mother could. Already I could hear her snoring across the hall. True to her word, nothing — not caffeine, not another murder, not even endangering her grandson — could prevent her from a good night's sleep.

Would strangling her while she snoozed wake her, do you suppose?

I must finally have dropped off, because when my eyes fluttered open it was nearly eight o'clock and sun was streaming in around the edges of the curtains. I felt that disorientation that often follows waking from a deep sleep, and it took me a moment to realize this was Saturday morning.

Enticing smells from below were wafting their way to me, like curling, beckoning fingers, drawing me out of bed like a sleepwalker. Sushi had since abandoned ship, no doubt "helping" Mother in the kitchen.

I tromped downstairs, teeth unbrushed, eyes rimmed with mascara, hair in such a disarray that any mouse in the house would have been happy to nest there.

I plopped down at the Duncan Phyfe dining room table, which had already been set. In addition to the green jadeite Fire King dishes, three little lidless antique glass salt cellars awaited, containing not salt but the daily medication of the home's three occupants: Mother's bipolar pill, my Prozac caplet, and Sushi's insulin, the filled syringe balanced ridiculously across her pill cup.

Mother breezed in carrying a plate of freshly baked Danish coffee cake cut into large squares. She was obviously working hard to get back in my good graces, perhaps sensing I'd only managed to drift off to sleep last night by fantasizing about choking her.

She knew the best way to try to make things up to me was through my stomach, knowing how much I loved that particular old family pastry.

KAFFE KAGE

For the Cake

1 cup plus 1 cup all-purpose flour
1/2 cup plus 1/2 cup butter
1 cup plus 1 Tablespoon cold water
3 eggs
1/2 teaspoon almond extract

For the Icing

1 Tablespoon butter
1 teaspoon almond extract
1 cup powdered sugar
Whole milk or cream, as needed
1/2 cup chopped almonds, for garnish

In a large bowl, place 1 cup of flour, then cut with 1/2 cup butter until texture is like coarse crumbs. Sprinkle with 1 Tablespoon cold water and toss with a fork until the mixture forms a ball. Roll out the ball onto a greased cookie sheet until 1/2 inch thick, and set aside.

Using an electric mixer, combine 1/2 cup softened butter with 1 cup cold water. Place in a saucepan and heat to boiling, remove from heat, and add 1 cup of flour all at once, stirring until smooth. Add the eggs, one at a time, beating well after each one. Add the 1/2 tsp. of almond extract and continue beating until the mixture is smooth.

Spread this mixture over the dough on the cookie sheet. Bake in a preheated oven at 400°F for 45 minutes, or until puffed and golden brown. Set aside.

For icing, combine the butter, almond extract, and powdered sugar in a bowl. Stir in enough milk to make the consistency to your liking. Spread this icing over the warm pastry and then sprinkle with chopped almonds.

Serves 10 to 12

Mother placed the plate in the middle of the table, went back to the kitchen, then returned with a carafe of coffee in one hand and a platter of scrambled eggs and crisp bacon in the other.

I regarded her suspiciously as she filled my cup to the brim.

"Eat up, dear," she said cheerily, sitting herself down, "while the food is still nice and hot."

"I'm not working at the store today, am I?" I asked. The Danish treat told me as much. Also, it told me that this wasn't because Mother wanted to lighten my work-load.

"No, dear," she said. "I've already called Joe in off the bench. You're needed at the Playhouse."

"And if I refuse to go to the Playhouse and take over as stage manager? Because that's what you have in mind, isn't it?"

She had the first full run-through scheduled this morning.

Mother nudged my little glass cellar with a finger. "Take your Prozac, darling. You're going to have to drive me out there anyway. . . ." She shrugged. "So you might as well stay. And I need your help desperately. *Somebody* has to fill in for Miguel!"

"Because he was murdered."

"Of course. Can you think of a better reason for him to be absent? This is just temporary, dear."

"Not for Miguel it isn't. *He* won't be back."

"True. But until I can properly line someone up, who better to step into his shoes?"

From what she'd told me last night, his shoes must be pretty damp.

"You are knowledgeable about the Playhouse," she said, "and you've performed many of those duties before, particularly when you and I have gone out and about to do my one-woman Shakespearean shows. Can you think of a better option?"

I popped the pill into my mouth and downed it with the coffee. "Yes. You should cancel."

"The run-through?"

"No! The play! You have a legitimate reason with losing Miguel. Announce that you will reschedule it for some other time, then do a different play. One you *hadn't* promised Gladys a lead role in. And then never get around to rescheduling the thing!"

Mother thought about that but shook her head. "I've never cancelled a play or a performance. The show must go on is not merely an expression."

True. For the entire run of *A Streetcar Named Desire,* Mother, as Blanche, hobbled around on crutches after she'd broken her leg, which she explained (in a line she added) came from having missed a running jump at the streetcar.

I sighed. "All right. I'll fill in, but *just* fill in, for today. You'll have to get someone else after that."

Her smile was dazzling, if not somewhat demented. She really hadn't made a bad Blanche. "That's my girl. Now eat up, child — we must leave, toot sweet!"

Actually, I knew my fate had been sealed

after we'd begun our conversation, because I'd made a crucial mistake — actually, two. I'd used the words *go* and *Playhouse* in Sushi's presence. And she'd already trotted off and come back with her leash, her tail enthusiastically wagging, her eyes wide and demanding.

Since Mother had left her Sheriff's Explorer parked at the jail, I used the C-Max for transportation. Mother was in civilian togs today.

Along the way she got a report by cell from Deputy Chen, who'd had contact with the Chicago PD, saying that Alek Wozniak was either in hiding or on the run, which made me feel better about Jake's safety, though not ours.

We were the first ones to arrive at the Playhouse. Inside, I let Sushi run free while I swung into my role as stage manager; as Mother indicated, I was not unfamiliar with the duties, having been volunteered into harness before.

First, I made sure the stage door was left unlocked, then went backstage and switched on only the lights that would be needed for rehearsal. This meant leaving the house lights off, keeping the auditorium seating in darkness, creating the atmosphere for this first run-through as much like that of a real performance as possible, minus only the songs, which would be rehearsed separately for now.

Next, I checked the stage. Sometimes all that needed to be done was mark the floor with tape to designate where rooms or areas were in a scene, but my late predecessor had already provided much more than that. In fact, the set, representing the apartment of Sally, was already mostly in place: center stage living room, bedroom to the right, kitchen to the left, all furnished with modern pieces, since Mother had reset the era from the 1940s to present day. The only thing lacking was the back wall with window and front door, which would be built and erected later.

Mother came up beside me. "As much as that young man irked me, he was a marvel as a stage manager."

I said, "I wonder what happened to him, and why."

She jangled a set of keys. "Wonder later, dear. Do you think it's easy for me to leave a murder inquiry in the wings? But one must compartmentalize in life. Now, I need you to go and get something for me. Out in the storage building."

I took my orders and the keys and left.

What Mother wanted was a time-worn

device she always used while directing in the dark from the middle section of the audience: a megaphone. Not a bullhorn with microphone, but the old-fashioned Rudy Vallée variety, a big cardboard cone with metal trim.

I'll pause for a moment to give you time to select an aspirin, ibuprofen, acetaminophen, or naproxen.

Ready? Did you take several good sips of water? All right. We'll proceed.

I managed to slip out of the stage door without Sushi tagging after and headed to the storage building. This time I went in through the oversize shed's front door, not the garage, and started toward where I thought the megaphone might be, in an area that had stools, clipboards, stopwatches, and other items that came in handy backstage.

Anyway, along the way, I began to notice that pieces of furniture I'd become familiar with — and that were grouped together according to their category — had either been moved elsewhere or were missing. I didn't dwell on what that might mean, my compartmentalized focus on the search for Mother's ridiculous Rudy Vallée–style megaphone.

Which I found, and took dutifully back to Mother.

When the three actors playing principals in *Voice* arrived — Kimberly and Zefross together, followed by Gladys — Mother did not mention the tragedy that had befallen Miguel.

She told me this was because his next of kin had yet to be contacted, and as sheriff she was following correct procedure. But I suspected it was mostly because the news might cast a pall on the rehearsal. She only told the players that I would be filling in for him this morning.

I won't bore you with details of the next three hours of the run-through, other than to say I was kept busy, logging running times, recording changes to the script, and noting the blocking. No prompting was required, because at this early stage the actors were "on book," scripts in hand. Or anyway, two of them were — Kimberly and Zefross.

Gladys was already "off book" — and letter perfect.

Even so, the bank teller's performance was not inspiring, to say the least, and typical of an untrained local actor. Not stinking up the joint, which was a relief, but not a revelation of hidden talent.

After the rehearsal, Kimberly and Zefross departed — I had a feeling they got together to go over more than just their lines — while Mother and Gladys sat alone on the stage couch. I stood off to one side, holding Sushi as if she were flowers I was waiting to deliver to the actress.

"I wasn't very good, was I," Gladys said morosely. "I could see the other two rolling their eyes."

Mother said kindly, "You'll make progress, dear, with every rehearsal. You have your lines down, and that's the first step. It's what every actor builds upon. Dear, you have it in you to become a good actress — I can feel it in my bones!"

That was not necessarily a good thing. Mother's bones were as brittle and porous as a coral reef sponge; she'd been given a prescription of Boniva for osteoporosis but hadn't taken the once-a-week-first-thing-in-the-morning pill, because she'd have to wait a half an hour afterward before drinking her coffee . . . which, in her words was, "a bridge too far."

Something occurred to me that didn't have anything to do with bad acting or brittle bones, either.

"Gladys," I said, stepping closer, "when you came into our shop last week, you mentioned you'd been out here Monday night."

"Yes?"

"And you said that there was a man over at the storage building. Could you see who it was?"

She shook her mousy brown mop. "No. It was too dark."

I stepped even closer. "How about vehicles? Was there a black Mazda? Or a red truck?"

Mother's eyes lit up as she changed compartments — she knew the Mazda was Miguel's and the truck Leon's.

"Sorry," Gladys said with a little shrug. "Guess I wasn't really paying much attention. Once I realized the Playhouse was closed, I left."

I asked, mildly annoyed, "Didn't it cross your mind this person might be a burglar?"

Gladys thought about that. "No . . ." she said. "Because I think he was putting something *in* the building, not taking something out."

Mother's eyes were on me. "Brandy, what are you getting at?"

I looked at her. "I didn't do an inventory or anything, but it appears to me like some prop furniture is missing out there — nice things, like that antique side table Mrs. Goldstein donated a few months ago."

That put color into Mother's cheeks, and

she turned to Gladys. "Dear! Would you agree to be hypnotized?"

The bank teller's eyes got big. "Hypnotized . . . whatever for?"

"To help you remember what you saw. After all, your eyes *did* see, even if your mind paid little heed."

"Golly, I've never been hypnotized before."

"Well, then, it will be a new and exciting experience for you, darling!"

"I don't know. . . . Is it that important?"

"Extremely," Mother said.

"You're the director," Gladys said.

Mother's budding actress followed us in her car back to Serenity, then to Tilda Tompkins's residence, a white two-story clapboard house with aging lattice work and paint-peeling boards that you might call shabby chic, if your emphasis was on the shabby. The bungalow was set back from the street, across from Greenwood, Serenity's oldest cemetery.

Since Sushi was along, my intention was to leave her in the car. But when Mother and I started to get out, doggie dearest threw a barking tantrum.

"There'll be *cats*," I advised Sushi. "You'll be outnumbered."

She understood the word *cat,* all right, but didn't back off.

"Okay, I warned you," I told the animal. "It'll be your fault when you get your face scratched."

On the wide, sagging wooden porch, Tilda greeted Mother, Gladys, and me as I held Sushi. Our hostess was on the far side of forty, and comfy there, slender, with long golden red hair, translucent skin, and a scattering of youthful freckles across the bridge of her nose. Tilda had a fondness for Bohemian clothing, and today she had on a white blouse, tan suede fringed vest, and long colorful patchwork skirt. Brown Birkenstock sandals completed the ensemble.

"You have arrived at an opportune time," she addressed Mother. "You've caught me in-between my Tantra Sex class and a new one I've just launched on mantras and mudras."

Mother smiled and asked, "How long having you been teaching mud wrestling?"

"No, Vivian — *mudras.* It's a meditation technique involving a silent form of chanting."

"My favorite style of chanting," Mother said, then gestured to Gladys. "This is the young woman I called you about."

Tilda acknowledged her new visitor with

266

a nod but was all business, stepping to one side and waving us through. "Come in, come in, one and all. I have only half an hour."

Gladys and Mother passed through the New Age portal, but I hesitated with Sushi.

With a peaceful smile, Tilda said, "I'm sure she'll be all right, Brandy. She probably already knows Mrs. Leggett, who will keep a watchful eye on her."

Mrs. Leggett had run the local pet store.

"Oh," I said, "how long has she been here?"

"Since yesterday! She's a new addition to our lodgers. She showed up at the back door. And it's only been three days since the funeral."

I followed the New Age guru inside.

The front room of Tilda's home was a combination living space, waiting room, and funky shop, a mystic area that included soothing candles, healing crystals, swirling mobiles of planets and stars, and a cash register. Like the Cinders, much was for sale here, but Tilda's items were priced.

And then there were the cats, which were *not* for sale — cats everywhere, filling the couch, seat cushions, back, and arms, curled on the half-dozen folding chairs and lounging on every window sill.

Each time I came, there were more cats. *Why?* you might well wonder, particularly you newbie readers. Certainly not because Tilda proactively acquired them — rather because people kept dying and being buried in the nearby cemetery, and those who couldn't otherwise cross over to the other side simply crossed the street as a spiritually inhabited cat. The tabbies came to Tilda for a place to live during their new incarnation — certainly not for the Tantra Sex class, mantras, and mudras.

Anyway, that's what Tilda Tompkins believed.

"Which one is Mrs. Leggett?" I asked.

"The fat kitty on the windowsill over there," Tilda said pointing.

The cat plopped down from its perch, waddled over, looked up at Sushi in my arms, and meowed. Several other cats joined Mrs. Leggett, while the rest seemed uninterested.

I lowered Sushi to the floor, hesitating, fearful that a fight might begin. When nothing happened but a collective purring from the felines, I shrugged and followed Tilda, who moved with ethereal, dreamy grace back through the kitchen to a small, dark claustrophobic room with a single shuttered window.

The only source of light came from a table lamp, its revolving shade with cutout stars sending its own galaxy swirling on the ceiling.

Gladys was already stretched out on the red velvet fainting couch, Mother seated on the small stool that I usually took, which left me standing in a corner by the door, since the only other seating was a chair next to the sofa, reserved for Tilda.

Tilda took her place, and Mother handed the guru a piece of paper, which the woman studied for a moment, then placed in her lap.

"Now, Gladys," Tilda began, "there's nothing to be afraid of — no matter what you may have seen stage performers and television charlatans do, I certainly won't make you cluck like a chicken."

The humorless Gladys merely said, "Thank you."

From the table with the lamp, Tilda took a long gold-chained necklace with a round, shiny disk, then dangled the necklace before Gladys's face and began to swing it like a pendulum.

"Watch the medallion," Tilda said slowly, softly. "Consider its gentle motion. Surrender to its gentle motion."

Mother's obstructed view behind Tilda

was no accident, as several times when she was present while the guru hypnotized others, Mother, watching the swinging necklace, had been hypnotized, too . . .

. . . to disastrous effect.

Out would pop people Mother had been in a former life, like Iras, handmaiden to Cleopatra, who was in charge of the Queen's asps; Matoaka, the younger sister of Pocahontas, and (she claimed) the real love of Captain John Smith's life; and Myles Carter, personal attendant to King George the Third, who convinced the monarch that any talk of revolution by the colonists was merely empty "poppycock." Helena Kowalski, Madame Curie's talkative cook, who insisted that she — not her employer — had come up with the idea of pasteurization, was a particularly hard genie for Tilda to get back into the bottle.

The guru was saying, "You feel relaxed . . . so very relaxed. You're getting sleepy . . . so very sleepy. Your eyelids are heavy . . . so very heavy . . . so heavy that you simply can't keep them open."

I looked over at Mother and her eyes were closed — maybe it was Tilda's voice and not the necklace that she had previously succumbed to! Before I could move to kick her, though, Mother's lids flickered open, and she was back among the currently living.

"I'm going to count backward from ten to one," Tilda said. "And when I say one, you will be asleep, completely, deeply asleep, and will respond to what I say. Ten . . . nine . . . eight . . ."

Gladys's body went limp at seven.

Tilda consulted the paper in her lap. "This past Monday night you visited the Playhouse and found the front doors closed. Is that right?"

"Yes."

"So you walked around the building to see if the stage door was open. Is that correct?"

"Yes."

"Someone is at the storage building. Can you see him?"

"No."

"You can't see him?"

"I can see *them.*"

Mother leaned forward and whispered into Tilda's ear, as this deviated from her script.

Tilda asked, "How many people do you see?"

"Two."

"Do you know who they are?"

"One is Miguel, the stage manager. The

other I've never seen before."

"Can you describe this person?"

Mother blurted, "Is it a man or woman?"

Tilda shushed her with a hand and repeated the question.

Gladys spoke in a slow, robotic way. "The person is wearing a baseball cap, so could be either male or female."

"And what are these two doing?"

"Taking things down off the back of a truck and putting them inside the building, then loading things up from out of the building."

Tilda looked back at Mother and whispered, "Anything more?" Mother took the paper, scribbled something on it, and handed it back.

Tilda read the note, frowned, shrugged, then said, "Gladys, I'm going to give you a *suggestion*. On the opening night of *Voice of the Turtle,* you are going to be the most successful actress who" — she peered at the note — "ever trod the boards?"

Mother nodded.

Tilda tried again, "Ever trod the boards."

I glared at Mother. Had this little impromptu prompt been in her mind all along? Was she operating out of two compartments with this one visit?

Disgusted, I quietly left the room.

In the living/waiting/shop room I found Sushi snuggled on the couch with Mrs. Leggett and other cats. She was like a sultan with his harem, except for being female and spayed. I sighed. With such a cushy life, why would any of them want to move on?

About five minutes later, the session having ended, Tilda, Mother, and Gladys came in.

Gladys was in a conversation with Mother. "No, I don't remember anything that happened, Mrs. Borne, during the hypnosis session. But I sure do feel rested. Was I of any help?"

"Indeed you were," Mother said.

"I'm so glad," Gladys replied, pleased to have pleased her director.

I pried Sushi away from her friends, then we exchanged thank-yous and good-byes, gave Tilda her modest fee, and left.

I walked to the C-Max and got inside with Sushi; Mother had a few words with Gladys on the sidewalk, they parted, the bank teller walked to her car — was that a spring in her step? — and Mother joined me.

I said, "Don't you think you should have been more specific?"

"About what the girl saw?"

"No. About becoming the most successful actress who ever trod the boards. Who are you expecting to show up? Katharine Hepburn? Helen Hayes?"

She twisted toward me. "Dear, the suggestion was only meant to be a confidence booster — I don't think Gladys is going to take it *literally*."

I raised my eyebrows as high as I could without their leaving my face.

Mother asked, "And so what if she does? There's nothing wrong with channeling the two you mentioned, or for that matter Sarah Bernhardt, Constance Bennett, or Patti LuPone."

"I doubt Gladys knows who *any* of them are."

"Regardless," Mother went on, "the suggestion probably won't stick anyway."

I started the engine. "Playhouse?"

"Playhouse."

Not wanting Sushi wandering around the storage building where there might be rat poison — or had that been a ruse to keep me out of the building? — we dropped her off home. Mother took the opportunity to get into her spare uniform.

So it was midafternoon when I pulled the C-Max up in front of the storage building. Mother used her set of keys to let us in, then switched on all the overhead lights.

"Show me," she commanded.

274

I led her to the area where the small furniture had been grouped.

"Yes," she said, eyes narrow. "Several things are missing from here." She cited Mrs. Goldstein's table and a Victorian-era lamp with beaded shade, which I hadn't noticed was gone.

And those two pieces were worth money, as Mother had frequently sought out (free) quality stage furniture and props, believing that if the performances were bad, at least the audience could enjoy looking at the fine decor.

I asked, "Do you think they were sold along with the vase?"

"Very possibly. It's my opinion that Miguel and Leon had been plundering valuable set props for who knows how long."

I asked, "And perhaps substituting other things in their place so the stock wouldn't look *too* depleted?"

"Possibly. We won't know until a full inventory is taken — which we will do ASAP."

Mother had turned away, and I followed her as she wandered the aisles, pointing out other missing antiques — and a few new pieces that had been added — which may or may not have been legitimate contributions. She couldn't be sure, because her job as sheriff had kept Mother out of the loop of acquisitions.

We had arrived at the back end of the building, where large, tall sections of a castle wall had been stored after a performance of *Camelot*.

Mother pointed to them. "Those set pieces used to be flat against the wall, but they've been put on casters and moved forward."

Creating a space behind them.

I wheeled one partition out far enough for us to slip behind it.

Mother surveyed the hidden area. "Just what I expected to find," she said.

"Me too," I said.

Antiques from the Wentworth mansion.

A TRASH 'N' TREASURES TIP

When selling an item at auction online, understand that buyers often wait until the last moment to bid, a practice called "sniping," which significantly increases the bidding price. Sometimes, before that happens, a seller will get discouraged and stop the auction or accept a low amount for their item. So be patient. Let the bidders be the anxious ones. Mother, for example, during the final hour of an auction, checks the bid-

ding every ten seconds. Could be worse.
Could be five.

CHAPTER ELEVEN:
IN WHICH VIVIAN
GOES OFF COURSE
AND BRANDY GETS TEED OFF

Of course, not all the Wentworth antiques had been hidden in the storage building at the Playhouse — notably missing were the distinctive lion's-head dining room table, chairs, and buffet, most likely left behind to be destroyed in the fire to make an insurance investigator believe (along with pieces of furniture posing as set props) that all had been a total loss.

But many of the antiques were here, including several Victorian bedroom sets, valuable accent tables, a few lamps, velvet-cushioned chairs, and wall pictures, including the oil portrait of little Arabella. All were appropriate items to be found in a theater's storage building, for use as set dressing.

While I took photos with my cell, Mother called Tony, informed him what we'd found, and asked him to send someone out here to check for fingerprints on susceptible surfaces, like the metal base of a lamp or the glass in a framed picture.

"I'm not staying on the scene," the sheriff informed the chief. "I have things to do. In the meantime, I'll leave the key on the top ledge of the side door."

I could hear Tony protesting, but Mother ended the conversation. When he rang back, she ignored him, shifting the phone to vibrate mode.

Turning toward me, she said, "Come, Brandy. I see a light at the end of the tunnel."

"A train?"

"No. A lit match."

On the way back to town, Mother accepted a call from Deputy Chen, which I was able to hear.

"Sheriff," Chen said, "Chief Cassato wanted me to tell you that Alek Wozniak has a reliable alibi for last night — whatever his actual role was in all this, he could *not* have driven to Serenity and killed Miguel."

"Interesting. Anything else?"

"Yes. We put a rush on the DNA from Leon's shaver. We got a match. That was your janitor's burned body in the Wentworth ruins, all right."

"*Very* interesting."

"And one last thing . . ."

"Yes?"

"The Chief said not to *ever* flipping ignore his call again."

"Well, that's cheeky of him."

"You should have heard it before I edited it."

"Ten-four."

Saturday afternoon typically meant another bridge game soiree at the country club, where Mother expected to find Evelyn Snydacker. This time around, Mother ignored the approaching Mr. Eggler, brushed passed him, tapping her badge as she did. Then she marched down the carpeted corridor as I trailed her.

In the main dining room, she spotted Evelyn at a table, strode over, grabbed her by the arm, hauled the woman out of her chair, and dragged her from the room like a child getting taken to the woodshed. Eyes and mouths all around the room were wide and round, at least on those ladies who could tear their eyes away from their cards.

In the empty bar, Mother plopped Evelyn rudely down in the chair the woman had occupied the other day.

"How *dare* you, Vivian Borne!" The president of the Historical Preservation Society was huffing and puffing with no house to blow down. "I was in the middle of a bid, I'll have you know!"

Mother jabbed at her with a finger. "You lied to an officer of the law!"

Evelyn reared back in confusion. "*What* officer of the law?"

Mother pointed at her badge again. "*This* officer of the law!"

"What are you *talking* about?"

Looming, Mother said, "You told me you were home the evening of the fire, but I have an eyewitness who saw you going into the Wentworth mansion around eight o'clock."

An invisible witness, but who was quibbling? Still, I couldn't quite picture Evelyn's lawyer cross-examining a vacant chair.

But, mea tulpa, Evelyn's demeanor changed, the bridge player's bravado collapsing like a house of cards.

The accused's eyes sought me out. "Get me some Scotch, will you? Straight up."

Nice to be serving a function.

I went behind the counter, poured several fingers of Johnnie Walker into a tumbler, and delivered it to our interview subject.

Evelyn downed the drink, then handed the tumbler back to me with a gesture that she wanted another. But Mother raised a "stop" hand and shook her head. She said to Evelyn, "You are lubricated enough, my dear. Spill."

The woman sighed, then stared past

Mother at nothing for a while. "All right. All right. I *did* go to see James that evening. I didn't mention it because I saw no reason to — after all, it wasn't anything important."

Mother said sweetly, "You might have left its relative importance up to me. What was the nature of your visit?"

"I told you, Vivian — it was nothing pertinent."

"Perhaps you'd be more comfortable if we had this little chat down at the station . . . although we don't serve alcohol there, I'm afraid."

"I . . . I'd prefer to talk here," Evelyn said, resigned. "I'll tell you the truth about the talk I had with James."

Which was this: Earlier that Monday, she had been going over the invoices of repairs on the mansion, material routinely turned in by Sutter to the society, as required by their bylaws.

And the woman noticed something she hadn't before. Many — but not all — of the billings were in the same hand. Checking them against personal letters and notes given to her by James suggested that the handwriting was his own.

Mother said, "He had been forging invoices."

Evelyn nodded. "For nonexistent repairs

282

and maintenance, and the materials they supposedly required."

"For how long?"

"For . . . years, I'm afraid. I've been much too trusting. This will cost me my presidency if word gets out, Vivian!"

"It's cost several lives already, and that's rather more serious than your social status. Go on."

A sigh. "I went over there and confronted James with the evidence. And he admitted that he'd been pocketing much of the grant money. When I said I was going to expose him, he laughed and said, 'No, you won't.' Can you imagine? Just like that." She paused. "He knew. He knew that if it got out, my reputation would be ruined right along with his. And not only that, but the reputation of the Historical Preservation Society would wear a stain we could never scrub out. We'd *never* be able to get another grant again. Who would trust us?"

"What then?"

A shrug. "I went home. I don't even remember driving, I was so upset."

Mother said, "And later, you arranged to meet James Sutter somewhere remote — and killed him."

The woman's eyes grew large. "You can't honestly believe that, Vivian! That I would be capable of *murder* . . . let alone burying his body in the woods somewhere. I can barely carry my groceries into the house!"

Mother let Evelyn sweat a few moments. Then she said, "I don't really think it's likely you're the murderer in this affair. But to prove that, I'll need a statement from you to the effect of what you've just told me — and anything else you remember about that visit."

Evelyn sat forward. "There *was* something. Something James said before I left the mansion. He said, 'If you'll just give me a little time, I have a plan to pay the money back. After that, I'll turn over a new leaf, and every invoice I give you will be legitimate.' I don't know whether that was a lie to help keep me quiet, or if he really had lined up a way out."

"He didn't elaborate?"

"No." She shrugged one shoulder. "But, obviously, whatever that way was? It didn't work out."

We found Gavin Sutter at home, working in the garage with the double-wide door rolled up. When I pulled into the drive, he spotted us and came out cleaning his hands on a rag.

Mother and I got out of the car, and I

tried to read his face, but it seemed set in stone.

"Sheriff," he said, rather flatly. "What brings you here?"

Mother got right down to business. "You were seen by a reliable witness going into your stepfather's house the night of the fire. Yet when we spoke the other day, you claimed not to have had any contact with him recently."

Gavin's jaw clenched, then unclenched. "Yes, I did see James that night." He took a deep breath, and exhaled. "I didn't mention it because I didn't want to lie to you."

"You preferred to lie by omission, then?"

"I guess that's a fair way to put it."

"Why the reticence?"

"My stepfather and I had . . . we'd had words."

"About?"

He was wiping his hands nervously on the rag now. "Cliff Reed told me my father-in-law had allowed the insurance policy on the mansion to lapse. You're aware I'm cosigner of the loan, putting me in a terrible place financially, should anything happen — which it did."

Mother asked casually, "Did that prompt you to kill him, or did you come to that decision later?"

Gavin's eyes got big and angry. "I *didn't* kill James! And I didn't have a damn thing to do with the fire or the body found in it. And that's all I care to say until I have my attorney present."

"That's your prerogative, *of course*," Mother said. "Still, it might improve your position if you were to be openly co-operative. Whatever bad words you may have had on your last meeting with James Sutter, however justified they might have been . . . he *was* your stepfather."

But he wasn't having any. He turned abruptly away, went inside the garage, and closed its door.

We returned to the C-Max.

After we got in, I asked, "Why didn't you tell Gavin that some of the antiques have turned up?"

"Because, dear, the news wouldn't affect him one way or the other." She gave me a narrow-eyed look. "Plus, I want to keep that information out of circulation for the moment, along with the identity of the burned body."

Mother placed a call to Cliff Reed's residence, where a cleaning woman told her that he could be found at the public golf course.

I pointed the car in that direction.

Serenity Municipal, Munie for short, was located along Highway 38 going west of town; the course had been steadily peeling away the swanky country club's members by offering considerably lower fees. Granted, Munie didn't have elegant evening dining, or a grand room for a wedding reception, or even a swimming pool; but that was fine for folks who chiefly cared about golfing (and their pocketbooks). A newly built clubhouse, along with an overall improved course, made the upstart even more attractive.

Inside the clubhouse, with its tasteful rustic decor, Mother was told she could find Cliff on the links, "probably out on the back nine."

Outside, I stood alongside Mother while she considered her next move. She seemed stymied until a golf cart carrying a middle-aged couple came wheeling our way en route to the first tee.

Mother stepped in front of the cart and spread her arms wide, and the man operating it slammed on the breaks.

"I'm commandeering this vehicle in the name of the law!" Mother announced to the startled pair.

When the couple just sat there frozen with their mouths open, Mother — for the third time today — tapped her badge. Then she waggled a thumb like a hitchhiker. "Out-ski!"

As they clambered off the cart, Mother commanded, rather like Adam West to Burt Ward (look it up), "Brandy, *hand* these good citizens their clubs!"

I rushed to the rear of the cart, grabbed the two bags, one at a time, and gave them to their open-mouthed owners.

"Chop chop!" the sheriff said.

I jumped in next to her.

Mother put pedal to the metal, and I glanced back at the astonished couple, gaping at us, not having uttered a single syllable. I gave them a shrug and a sympathetic smile.

Munie, after spending a small fortune on improving each hole, had installed golf cart paths to protect them. But using these paths to reach the back nine would have taken us in a roundabout way. So Mother travelled as the crow flies, heading across the fairways at a fifteen-miles-per-hour clip, the maximum speed the small gas-powered vehicle could muster.

Since it had rained heavily during the night, and because many of the courses were hilly, the cart left behind track marks, especially going up an incline, where the tires pressed into — occasionally *dug* into — the grass.

But Mother paid no heed, barreling down the fairways, disrupting play and creating chaos while yelling, "Fore!" and "Playing through!"

"This thing," she said at one point, hunkered over the wheel, "could really use a siren."

As we approached the thirteenth hole, Mother said, "Eureka! There's our man!"

Cliff was on the green, bent over, getting ready to putt, his concentration rivaling that of Tiger Woods; his male playing partner stood several yards away, holding the flagstick, frozen in the stillness. Even the birds seemed to be respecting the silence.

Then, just as Cliff was taking his shot, Mother called out, "Oh, *yoo*-hoo!" and the ball missed the cup by a mile. Figurative mile.

He looked up, annoyed at first, then with alarm as the cart leapt up onto the green and came to an abrupt stop, the tires creating more damage than any pitch mark or divot could ever manage — and there wasn't a golf tool made that could fix that.

Mother hopped out. "Mr. Reed! I'm so glad I ran across you."

She almost had.

He frowned. "How did you know where I was?"

"A little birdie told me," Mother said. Then she laughed and added, "A little golfing joke." But no one else was even smiling, much less laughing.

Stiffly angry, he said, "My *cell* wouldn't have sufficed?"

"Oh, no," Mother said, approaching him. "I wanted to deliver some good news in person." She looked at the partner. "Oh, hello, Walter. Fine day to be out on the links, don't you think?"

Walter, a middle-aged banker, said, "Fine day, Vivian."

"Well?" Cliff asked impatiently, drawing Mother's attention back.

"You will no doubt be pleased to learn," she said, "that the Wentworth antiques were not entirely lost in the mansion fire. A good number of pieces have been found in the storage building at the Playhouse. Isn't that wonderful? Apparently, someone had switched them with stage props."

Mother's magnified eyes behind her large glasses studied his response.

"Well, yes," Cliff replied. "That *is* good news." But his expression did not reflect his words.

"I *thought* you might be pleased," Mother

said, as if he'd been effusive. "Now the insurance company won't have to pay out a million smackeroos, and Benjamin Wentworth hasn't lost his ancestral heritage — what's left of it, with the mansion gone." She paused. "Of course, there'll be an investigation into how those antiques wound up at the Playhouse . . . and an inquiry into any false claims that may have been perpetrated on the insurance company."

I didn't expect his reaction.

Cliff dropped his putter and walked away.

"Mr. Reed!" Mother called after him. "I've not yet finished!"

But he kept on going, his pace picking up, heading to a golf cart that was parked on the path.

Mother whipped out her cell, called for backup, then sprinted to our cart. Hopping in, she said, "Brandy, best I drive solo."

She gestured for me to get out, which I gladly did, not wanting to participate in what I thought might happen next.

"Sorry, dear," she called, driving off, "the extra weight would only slow me down!"

Extra weight! I was madder at her than Cliff . . .

. . . who had reached his cart and was doing a U-turn to head back toward the clubhouse, where his car would no doubt be waiting. This gave Mother time to cut him off, forcing the man to drive onto the course, where she took hot pursuit. Or as hot as two vehicles going fifteen miles per hour can get.

I watched with Walter at my side as Mother caught up with Cliff, ramming her cart into his, again and again, bumper-car style, then chasing him in circles, their tires digging up sod. This went on for a while. It might help to imagine "Yakety Sax" playing, Benny Hill–style.

"Well," the man said, "that's not something you see at Munie every day."

I shrugged. "Par for the course with Mother."

He looked at me.

I looked at him and said, "Another little golfing joke."

Walter frowned. "What did Cliff do to deserve that, anyway?"

"Oh, I'm not sure anybody deserves what Mother serves up. She just wanted to ask him some questions."

"Huh. Interesting way to conduct official business."

A police car, lights flashing, siren going, arrived via the cart path, and officers Munson and Hansen got out. They stood for a moment as if trying to make sense of the tableau, then moved in and put a stop to it.

I wasn't near enough to hear any conversation, but after a few minutes Munson walked the handcuffed insurance agent back to the squad car, Hanson bringing up the rear.

Mother returned to the green in the commandeered golf cart, its sides dented, plastic roof askew.

"Hop in," she said to me, and to Walter, "Have a nice day!"

I said to him, "Your tax dollars at work," and threw him a wave. He waved back, rather numbly.

Using the cart path this time, we returned to the clubhouse, where the manager met us along with the owners of the cart. They crowded around, a three-person angry mob. Mother listened to their complaints patiently for a good fifteen seconds before saying, "Noted!"

And climbed out of the cart. I got out, too, as we abandoned our ride and made for the parking lot, amid shouts — from the manager: "You've ruined the course!"; from the husband: "You're going to pay for a new cart, you lunatic!"; and from the wife: "Honey, your blood pressure!"

In the C-Max, Mother instructed me to go to Benjamin Wentworth's condo, the "toot sweet" implied by her tone, and as I drove, she placed a call to the Reliable Hauling Company.

Ten minutes later, on the upper floor of the Grand Hotel, Mother's persistent bell-buzzing seemed to say the owner wasn't in.

But then the door flew open.

"What?" Wentworth said, with a good deal of irritation. He was dressed in a dark gray suit with lighter gray shirt and silver tie, as if about to go out to a business meeting. No sweats today, though I had a hunch he'd soon be sweating.

"Might I come in?" Mother asked.

"Not a good time," he said. "I have an appointment coming up soon. So say what you have to say, Vivian, right here."

"Oh," she said, her expression as sympathetic as only an expert bad actor could achieve, "I think you should sit down for this."

He sighed. "Well, all right. But you'll have to make it quick."

And he stepped aside.

I followed in Mother's footsteps, wishing she were a tulpa and I were her imaginary daughter.

In the living room area, the oriental rug had been rolled up, the bookshelves stood

vacant, and sealed boxes were stacked everywhere.

Wentworth turned to Mother, his expression accusatory. "What is this about, Vivian?"

"Specifically, it's about most of the antiques thought to have been lost in the fire
turning up stashed at the Playhouse. Apparently set props had been substituted for
them at the mansion, to leave remnants after
the blaze, designed to fool the insurance
company and fire investigators."

Wentworth's manner shifted to confusion.
"Who on earth would have done that? And
for whatever reason?" Then: "Oh! I follow.
Someone planned to 'fence' the pieces."

"Possibly," Mother said. "Or keep them
for himself. At any rate, there will be no
insurance payout now."

The man moved to an armchair. "You're
right at that, Sheriff. I *do* need to sit down."
He did so, then said, "Frankly, I can't say
I'm happy about this discovery, feeling as I
do about those wretched things, which
aren't really to my taste." He sighed. "I will
likely sell most of them. I suppose now I'll
have to make arrangements to have them
taken to the new house in Arizona."

Mother stepped closer. "Oh, but haven't
you already?"

"Already what?"

"Made those arrangements. And I don't think you plan to sell the antiques, but to furnish your new, big home with them. *You* grew up with those things all around and, despite what *you've* said, they meant a great deal to *you.*"

He batted that away. "Supposition. Sheer supposition. There's no proof of any of this."

"Oh, but there is. You see, I've been talking to the Reliable Hauling Company . . . and it seems their contract with you was to make *two* pickups — one here, and another at the Playhouse."

Wentworth didn't say anything, just covered his face with a hand. His words were muffled yet not difficult to make out at all.

He asked, "How did you know?"

"It was the painting, dear," Mother said. "The portrait of little Arabella that gave you away. Who else would want it? It wasn't particularly good, or by a known artist. You shouldn't have been that sentimental."

That last was a quote from *Vertigo,* one of Mother's favorite movies. At least she didn't utter it in her Jimmy Stewart impression.

Words filtered from between the man's fingers. "How . . . however did I get to this point?"

That was a rhetorical question, of course,

and an existential one. But Mother, despite her artistic bent, was first and foremost a pragmatist.

So she answered him.

"One step at a time," Mother replied. "The first step being when you saw an opportunity to have a million dollars *and* the antiques you really *did* care about, in spite of what you'd said, to fill that new home — a home far enough away from Serenity that you felt safe to have those precious items on display. And so what if someone from Serenity should visit? Why, these were similar pieces you found to replace the precious originals — perhaps even replicas." She paused. "The second step? That was joining with James as his accomplice in destroying the mansion."

"I didn't set the fire," he protested.

"No, but you knew *James* was going to." She paused. "I've always wondered about that lumber company fire, when Jimmy was employed there. Had there been an arrangement between you two back then, too? Sort of an unwitting trial run for the mansion swindle?"

"That's ridiculous," Wentworth said, stiffening, hands in his lap now as fists. "There was never any suggestion of arson at the lumber company."

"No. It's only my suspicious mind that thinks you saw a way out of a family-owned firm that had been losing money for years to the big chain lumber outfits. And Jimmy, knowing he'd eventually be out of a job there, was only too willing to help out, for a portion of the insurance money. It worked once — why not twice?"

Wentworth said nothing.

Mother, just throwing it out there, asked, "Did you know that James was going to kill Leon Jones before setting the fire?"

"No! I only found out about that after —"

Wentworth clammed up.

"I haven't Mirandized you," Mother said. "Until I do, nothing you tell me can be used in court."

Of course I was a witness who could report whatever he said — I was just ex officio, remember? And she darn well knew it.

He said, softly, "I didn't find out about Leon until after Miguel told me."

"Go on," Mother said.

His eyes were lowered, as if his memory were down there somewhere for him to retrieve. "Miguel came over here that night, about four in the morning, banging on the door. Said James had double-crossed us. You see, I was supposed to get the insurance money and all of the antiques that I

298

wanted, while Miguel and Leon would be paid a flat fee to help move the antiques out. That's the extent of my involvement." He paused. "But then, according to Miguel anyway, when the last of the antiques had been loaded into the truck, James hit Leon with a fire poker."

Mother was nodding. "James planned to 'die' in the fire, and then to disappear."

He was deep in debt, after all, and had been stealing the grant money.

"That would seem to have been his plan," Wentworth said. "And by having been made an accomplice, Miguel had no choice but go along with it. Miguel drove James to Leon's trailer to hide out. James had tickets for a flight leaving the country the following day."

Mother said, "What busy little bees you all were. But the situation only got worse, didn't it?"

"I . . . I'm not saying any more."

"Then I'll say it for you. You went to the trailer to confront James, things got out of hand, you killed him and buried his body in the woods."

Wentworth fell into a brooding silence.

Mother began pacing. "Perhaps you felt you would be down in Arizona by the time James was found — or maybe not found at all — but then I complicated things by mentioning that the Tiffany lava vase had surfaced for sale at a shop in Chicago. Well, that must have been unwelcome news! How many more of the antiques that should have been left behind in the fire had Miguel secretly siphoned off?"

Mother stopped pacing and faced Wentworth.

She said, "Then you seized an opportunity to kill Miguel — who, after all, could implicate you — when he asked for help in getting rid of Leon's truck. Only Miguel didn't know *he* would be going into the pit as well!"

Nothing from Wentworth. Perhaps he'd stopped listening. None of this was news to him.

Finally he spoke: "I want to call my lawyer."

"You can do that from the station, Mr. Wentworth," Mother said. "Your legal representation can explain to you all about what happens when you play with fire. It's one of those rare times when the literal and figurative converge."

A TRASH 'N' TREASURES TIP
It's important how you list something for sale on eBay when your word allotment is

300

limited, because searches are done by item titles instead of descriptions. For example, listing, "Lovely green medium-size bowl in good condition" will not give you as many hits as "Fire King jadite bowl, 8.25″ diameter, no chips." The accompanying photo of the item is important as well. Just as in the Wentworth case, a picture is worth a thousand words.

Chapter Twelve:
In Which Vivian Gets
Her Just Desserts
and Brandy Takes the Cake

The following morning, Mother, Tony, Deputy Chen, and I were squeezed into her small office at the county jail. She held court from behind her desk with Tony and the deputy in the visitor chairs opposite. Meanwhile, I half sat on a small metal file cabinet.

This was Mother's "wrap-up" meeting — just like the end of nearly every episode of her beloved *Perry Mason* TV series, when Perry and Paul and Della would tie up the loose ends over cups of coffee. In this case, the coffee had been carted over by yours truly from Elly's Tea Shop, along with a half dozen of her wonderful homemade fruit-filled white-icinged croissants, both apple and cherry. (Elly, nice though she is, would not share the recipe. Sorry!)

Benjamin Wentworth was currently oc-cupying a private cell elsewhere in this building, being held for the murders of

James Sutter and Miguel Ricardo; his arraignment was scheduled for later today. Tire-track casts, taken at both Leon's trailer (where James had been hiding out) and the gravel pit (where Miguel had been killed) matched the tires on Wentworth's Mercedes.

Clifford Reed had been questioned about his possible involvement in the scheme to defraud the insurance company (which he denied through his lawyer) and released pending further investigation by the police department. This was likely temporary, in part because insurance investigators would soon be scrutinizing the claim for possible fraud.

Evelyn Snydacker was also questioned regarding her knowledge of the invoices made by James, and — other than receiving unwanted publicity for herself and the Historical Preservation Society — was unlikely to suffer any further repercussions.

Gavin Sutter was cleared of any criminal involvement, the stepson having more to lose than gain by the destruction of the mansion, whose policy had lapsed.

Rocking back in her swivel chair, Mother asked, "Anything yet on the cause of the fire?"

"Still inconclusive," Tony said with a

shrug. "But evidence points to the living room and the use of gasoline."

Nodding, Deputy Chen said, "Not very imaginative, maybe, but that approach would insure the most destruction. And wasn't the bedroom, where Leon was found, directly above?"

"It was indeed," Mother said. Then, to Tony: "Speaking of fire and destruction, you said you had information on that propane tank that gave me a nasty surprise."

The chief shrugged again. "Apparently that was an accident."

"Really?" Mother asked. "No one meant to do me GBH?" She seemed disappointed. GBH, by the way, is Grievous Bodily Harm — she watches a lot of U.K. crime shows.

Tony went on, "Seems a faulty lamp in the bedroom sparked a fire that went through the trailer's back wall right next to the tank, which had a leak in the service valve. Didn't take much."

I looked at Mother. "I don't remember a light being on in the bedroom when we arrived to look for Leon."

She returned the look. "It wasn't. I turned the lamp on when I went back there to make a more thorough search."

Tony shifted in his chair. "On another note? I got the report from the Chicago PD on their interview with Alek Wozniak. You were right on the money, Vivian, about Miguel having contacted Leon's old cellmate to sell the vase." He shook his head, smiled ruefully. "Miguel's mistake was selling the vase to an antiques store instead of a fence. Brandy's noticing it on the Internet started everything to unravel."

I would have said, "You're welcome," just to get Mother's goat a little, if only my mouth hadn't been full of cherry croissant.

Deputy Chen swung toward Tony. "What's going to happen to the Wentworth antiques?"

"May I?" Mother asked.

"Be my guest, Sheriff," Tony replied with a wave of a hand.

"Charles," she said, "do you remember me mentioning that Jimmy's late wife, Diane, is a shirttail relation of the Wentworths?"

"Yes," the deputy said, nodding.

"Well, since Benjamin has no direct heirs, and his young wife very likely knew about the stolen furniture, and will be lucky not to be hauled in as an accomplice before or after the fact . . . I'm betting the swag will go to Diane's side of her family."

Chen said, "Something poetic about that."

Everyone agreed, including yours truly,

who was on the verge of getting reckless by following a cherry croissant with an apple one.

The police chief and the sheriff seemed on the same page, for once. But, as they say in books (like this one), little did I know. . . .

Let us fast-forward three weeks to the opening night of *The Voice of the Turtle.* Word had gotten around that Mother had had her way with the dialogue, as well as turning the play into a musical. So every seat in the auditorium was filled, all and sundry waiting in anticipation for the spectacle that was surely to follow.

Even though Mother had taken on a new stage manager, I opted to help out backstage rather than sit out in the audience. I'd witnessed rehearsals, suffering through Mother's risible rewrites of public domain songs and Gladys's stilted amateur-night-at-Dixie performance, and did not care to watch Mother face the humiliation she had caused herself. Or maybe I just dreaded the guilt by association. . . .

Cue the overture!

A medley — played adequately by a combo of trumpet, clarinet, bass, and drums — of "I'm Just Wild About Harry," "Toot, Toot, Tootsie," "April Showers," "Beautiful

Dreamer," "The Bells of St. Mary's" — concluded with a rousing rendition of "Alexander's Ragtime Band." Al Jolson and Bing Crosby fans should be giddy already.

Curtain up.

Polite applause, as Sally (Kimberly) manically rushes around straightening her apartment, while she rehearses aloud a scene from *Romeo and Juliet.*

The doorbell rings, a guest has arrived — her sexy pal Olive, Gladys making her first non-banking-lecture public appearance . . . her debut in a key role in a play.

Despite Mother's coaching, and the assistance of a platinum blond wig and sexy wardrobe, the bank teller's acting had not improved over these weeks. Watching from the wings, I held my breath, certain that the inevitable stage fright would take the woman from mediocrity to catastrophe.

Sally opens the door, greets her friend, but Olive just stands there frozen, an odd expression on her face. Had Gladys forgotten her simple first line? I see Mother, hidden behind the prop wall, about to feed the two words to her when, suddenly, magically, Olive seems to transform physically, now taller, oozing confidence, as she speaks the few words, then saunters provocatively into the apartment, one hand on a swaying hip.

Sally asks how her friend is, and after Olive reports that she's good, she adlibs in a Mae West manner, "But when I'm bad, I'm better."

The audience — mostly unfamiliar with the play — looks on in surprised delight. Seen from my vantage point in the wings, Mother merely looks surprised.

Kimberly, to her credit, stays in character, continuing on with her dialogue, although I could detect confusion in her eyes.

Olive takes in the apartment, delivers her line about how big it is, then adlibs again, "And you *know* how I like 'em *real* big."

Which brought a few chuckles from the house.

When Sally laments that she hasn't been able to get ahold of her actress friend for a while, Olive says that's because she's been busy performing split weeks and one-night stands. Then Olive/Gladys adlibs again, rolling her eyes upward, "Did I *mention* one-night stands?"

Some real laughs now.

Mother was next to me, hiss-whispering in my ear. "What's she doing?"

I whispered back, "What you *told* her to do."

"I never told Gladys to impersonate Mae West!" She was frowning, but in confusion.

"Although, I have to admit she's doing an astonishingly good job of it."

Then it came to me.

I whispered to Mother, "Remember the suggestion Tilda gave Gladys under hypnosis? At your bidding? I *told* you that you should have been more specific. Mae West probably *was* the most successful actress ever to 'trod the boards'!"

Mother moaned. "Why couldn't the girl have gone with Bette Davis, or Meryl Streep, or Bernadette Peters?"

More laughter was coming from the audience.

"No idea," I said. "But Mae West sure seems to be stealing the show."

Mother grew thoughtful. "This isn't what I had in mind . . . but I'll settle. And you're right about Mae West — she *was* a successful stage actress. Even wrote her own plays."

"Well, she's rewriting a lot of this one."

Rather than give you, the reader, a play-by-play of the rest of the play, I think the reviewer for the *Serenity Sentinel* summed it up rather well in the paper the next morning.

THE VOICE OF . . . MAE WEST?
by Sheila Walden

A ground-breaking performance of *The Voice of the Turtle* was given last night at the Serenity Playhouse to a packed house. Sheriff Vivian Borne, the director, took breathtaking liberties with the old warhorse of a play, bringing it into the twenty-first century, updating the out-of-fashion and sometimes politically incorrect dialogue, plus (gasp) adding musical numbers. While there sometimes seemed to be two different plays going on — a straight love story between characters Sally and Bill; and a wacky comedy with Sally's best friend, Olive — this critic admits to being conflicted on whether the strategy worked or not. But the audience seemed to love it.

Familiar old songs — with new Vivian Borne–penned lyrics (!) — were scattered throughout, and while the three principals gave Beyoncé and Johnny Legend little to worry about, their very amateurishness only added to the play's cock-eyed charm. Was this a stroke of genius by the notoriously eccentric director, or early onset dementia?

Kimberly Summers, a familiar staple of the Playhouse, gave a nice performance as Sally, while Zefross Jackson, playing Bill, brought realism as a vet home on leave from Afghanistan.

But it was newcomer Gladys Gooch who stole the show, playing her part à la Mae West, complete with ad-libbed, double entendre lines, some sassily spoken as asides to the delight of the audience (my favorite, "I used to be Snow White, but I drifted."). When Miss Gooch was not on-stage, the play occasionally lagged, while everyone waited for the delightful actress to reappear. She has a great future ahead of her, so a change in name might be considered.

The estate of the late John Van Druten was contacted about the changes made to the play, and a brief statement was issued through their lawyer: "No permission was given for any changes to the play, and further productions not in compliance with the original material will be swiftly met with legal action."

Ouch. So it appears that what happened last night at the Playhouse *stays* at the Playhouse . . . and in the memories of those fortunate enough to have seen it.

Mother, having read the review out loud, folded the paper.

We were in the dining room, seated at the Duncan Phyfe table, enjoying a leisurely Sunday brunch of Danish smorgasbord — cold meats, shrimp and herring, cheeses, and thinly sliced buttered bread. Plus coffee, of course.

"Well," Mother said, looking pleased. "I think the *Sentinel* has redeemed itself with that intelligent review, after panning me in the past."

"Really?" I said. "Some of those compliments were pretty left-handed. Your sanity seemed to be questioned, for example."

"Even the best reviews often have a barb or two. Anyway, I think I came off quite well, as did the play." She frowned. "Too bad the Van Druten estate put the kibosh on future productions. I think *my* version could have gone all the way to Broadway."

Or a courtroom.

Mother shrugged. "But that's their loss. In revenue, I mean." She smiled. "After all, it's still available."

"How is it still available?" I slipped Sushi a piece of cheese beneath the table.

Mother's eyes gazed ceilingward. "Why, it's up in the clouds, dear."

"Cloud. One cloud, and it's not even a real cloud. So — you had the performance recorded and uploaded?"

312

Her smile meant to be enigmatic and wasn't. "Let's just say I may have anticipated problems. Joe did quite a nice job from the balcony with his little HD camera."

"You'll have to take it down."

She gestured grandly. "Too late for that — by now it's spread beyond the clouds, to the sun, and the moon and the stars. A rather nice analogy, don't you think?"

The doorbell rang.

"That'll be Tony," I said, pushing back my chair. "He texted me he was dropping by."

I went out through the living room to let him in, Sushi beating me there, pawing at his legs as soon as he'd stepped in.

On his day off, Tony was casually dressed, jeans and a navy sweatshirt, but neither had a wrinkle or frayed thread. Even his tennies looked new. Why did such a perfect man put up with imperfect me? Although he gave me a smile, something behind it stopped me from giving him any more than a quick kiss.

Tony stooped and picked up Sushi, who then licked his face, not caring that something was behind his smile.

"Had lunch?" I asked.

"Late breakfast," he said. "But I'll take coffee."

"No problem."

I led the way to the dining room, where the chief greeted the sheriff, then he sat across from her.

"Quite a nice review," Tony said, nodding at the folded paper resting on the table. "I'm sorry I had to work through the evening and miss it."

Mother chirped, "Oh, but you can still see it — *ouch!*"

My foot had found its way to her shin.

Tony's eyebrows drew together. "Where can I see it?"

Mother cleared her throat. "Why, you can picture it perfectly in your mind's eye, if you'd like me to give you a detailed rendition, which I'm happy to do."

"Perhaps later," he said, distracted.

I handed Tony a cup of coffee with a little cream and sugar.

Mother, sensing now that his visit wasn't entirely a social one, asked, "Something on your mind, Chief?"

He took a sip, then set the cup down. "Yesterday, Commissioner Gordon called me to his office. Seems he's very unhappy with you, Vivian."

"Oh, really?" Mother asked innocently. "Why would that be?"

Tony gave her a hard stare. "You know why. The damage to the municipal golf course, which the county will have to pay for, is just the start."

Mother waved a hand. "Oh, that. Many a community has to pay for tidying up after a high-speed chase."

"Speaking of high-speed chases — at around fifteen miles per hour? — there's the little matter of a golf cart you damaged beyond repair. The personal property of Mr. and Mrs. Clyde Van Dusen?"

She frowned. "Van Druten, you say?"

"Van *Dusen.*"

Another dismissive wave. "That vehicle was an antiquated model. The county will see that they get a new one. Happy outcome all around."

Tony went on: "And there's your breaking into Leon's trailer —"

"I had probable cause," Mother interrupted. "He hadn't shown up for work."

Tony was shaking his head. "Not cause enough. If his truck had been there and he hadn't answered the door, then possibly you could justify it."

Mother grunted. "What else?"

"How about your manhandling Evelyn Snydacker at the country club?"

"Well," Mother said defensively, "she *lied* to me!"

"That's no excuse for dragging her from

315

the room by the arm in front of dozens of witnesses."

"Is she pressing charges?"

He paused, then admitted, "No . . . but that kind of behavior is unacceptable coming from a law enforcement officer."

Mother drew herself up. "Chief Cassato, I *was* trying to solve several murders at the time, as you may recall. And if a few rules got bent, and some toes got stepped on, well . . . it's nothing that can't be fixed."

"I'm afraid that isn't the case. This time, too much has happened for there to be *any* fix."

I'd been quiet until now. "What are you saying?"

He glanced at me, then back at Mother. "The county board of supervisors is recommending impeachment."

Mother frowned. "Can they do that?"

"They can. You're an elected official."

"And my odds of weathering that indignity?"

The chief didn't answer.

Mother stood slowly, then crossed to the windows facing the backyard, where she stood gazing out.

A full minute passed while Tony and I exchanged puzzled looks.

Then Mother turned to us. "You know,

producing that play made me realize just how much I missed the thee-ah-tah. The roar of the grease paint, the smell of the crowd! It's always been my life's blood. And, quite frankly, this job as sheriff has not been what I thought it would be . . . what with all the written reports, and official duties, and constraining rules and regulations that hamper my investigations."

Mother was a formidable poker player, and knew when to hold 'em.

And when to fold 'em.

She returned to the table and sat. "Perhaps certain arrangements could be made, Chief Cassato. The county might possibly not wish to go through the embarrassment of an impeachment, which I would fight and would most certainly survive — remember Teflon Bill!"

Quietly, Tony asked, "What kind of arrangements did you have in mind?"

"I would take early retirement."

Her reign had been only four and a half months.

Tony barely nodded. "Anything else?"

"A retirement party."

"I think that's doable."

"Plus, I'm to be given an honorary position as a county deputy, with no pay and no duties, of course, but a special badge."

He squinted at her. "What kind of special badge?"

I quipped, "Like the ones *The Wizard of Oz* gave out?"

"Very droll, Brandy," Mother replied. "No. Something honorary that holds authority, so people think they have to answer my questions, even if they technically don't. Something I can brandish by way of an I.D. in the unlikely event that I might at some future date become involved as an amateur sleuth in, say, a murder investigation."

Tony looked skeptical. "That kind of 'special duty' thing is done in big cities like L.A. and Chicago."

"That's right."

"Usually under corrupt circumstances."

"We'd be an exception, then, wouldn't we?"

The two poker players studied each other.

Finally Tony said, "Okay, Vivian. Anything else?"

"I get to keep the Vespa that was ordered for me."

He frowned. "You're pushing it, Vivian."

"Whether that's the case or not would depend."

"On?"

"Whether you think it's a fair trade for getting me to step down from my office."

He sighed. "I'll present your conditions to the board of supervisors."

Mother sat back with a satisfied look. "Well, then, off you go, before I change my mind."

He stood. "Vivian, you were a trial to deal with as a sheriff. You were frankly a trial *before* you were sheriff too. But you know what?"

"What, dear?"

"You're a hell of a detective."

She beamed at him. "I know, Chiefie dear."

I accompanied Tony to the front door, where we turned to each other.

"Please, please," I begged, "make this happen. Please don't put her . . . don't put me . . . through the ordeal of an impeachment proceeding."

"I thought you *wanted* her to be impeached."

"I want her out of that job, but not . . . humiliated."

His smile was a lovely thing. "I will push her demands through . . . if I have to throw the party, forge a badge with my bare hands, and buy the damn Vespa myself."

Then his voice softened and a hand came to my shoulder.

"Come to dinner at the cabin," he said.

"I'll take care of everything, including dessert."

"Okay," I said with a smile. "See you tonight."

We kissed, a long, lingering kiss that held the promise of better times ahead.

Tony's cabin was about five miles north of town along River Road, which followed the curves of the Mighty Mississippi. I turned left down the familiar narrow lane, then came to a stop behind Tony's car, parking in front of the rustic, slightly oversized log cabin.

Sushi, head over paws for Tony's dog, Rocky, had begged her way along, and she scrambled out of my door the second I'd opened it.

A few half-cut logs for steps led to a wide porch, where two birchwood rockers kept company with some potted plants. Sushi scratched at the front door as I knocked, and Tony opened it, wearing his idea of dressy casual — polo shirt and tan slacks.

"You look nice," he commented on my choice of a sweater, gauzy full skirt, short suede boots, and combed hair.

"I clean up pretty good," I said.

Tony stepped aside and Sushi went in first, making a beeline for Rocky, a large mixed breed with a circle around one eye, who knew the drill: flop down on his side and let Soosh crawl all over him until she tuckered herself out.

It had been several weeks since I'd been at the cabin, thanks to my deputy-daughter duties, and I'd missed its pleasant woodsy smell.

The inside was roomier than you'd think from the outside, with both a cozy area consisting of a fireplace, currently crackling with logs, an overstuffed brown couch, and a recliner, plus a dining area near the front windows with a four-chair round oak table and small china hutch.

The log walls displayed various collections of Tony's — ancient snowshoes; old fishing creels, rods, and nets; and framed photos of fishermen and hunters, sepia shots of days gone by.

The kitchen was just off the dining area, and from it wafted wonderful aromas.

"What's on the menu?" I asked.

"Caesar salad, potato pave, Dover sole with mustard hollandaise sauce, and lemon cake with butter-cream icing."

My eyes grew big. "You made all *that*?"

"No. That new French restaurant downtown. Picked it up after work."

We both laughed. Well, he chuckled, while

I sounded like a mule braying. A delicate one, of course.

Soon, with dusk settling in outside, we were enjoying the delicious meal, bathed in the flickering warmth of the fireplace, our light conversation going everywhere and nowhere — but nothing about his work or Mother. That was an unofficial rule out here.

As the windows grew dark, and dessert was about to be served, Tony lit a candle in the center of the table.

When I protested being too full to eat anything more, suggesting the cake be saved for later, he gave me a little smile and shook his head.

Tony disappeared into the kitchen, came back with the cake with pale yellow icing, and placed it in front of me. Written on it in red icing, in his own cursive hand, was *Will you marry me?*

And, girly-girl that I am, I burst into tears. He took me in his arms and led me gently away from the table.

That night, we never did get around to eating the cake.

A TRASH 'N' TREASURES TIP
For repeat sales, keep in touch with your best customers. Mother adds them to her

ever-growing Christmas letter list, from which the only escape is moving with no forwarding address or, perhaps, dying. And even then, Mother would investigate, if the circumstances were at all suspicious.

ABOUT THE AUTHORS

Barbara Allan is a joint pseudonym of husband-and-wife mystery writers Barbara and Max Allan Collins.

Barbara Collins made her entrance into the mystery field as a highly respected short story writer with appearances in over a dozen top anthologies, including *Murder Most Delicious, Women on the Edge, Deadly Housewives,* and the best-selling *Cat Crimes* series. She was the coeditor of (and a contributor to) the best-selling anthology *Lethal Ladies,* and her stories were selected for inclusion in the first three volumes of *The Year's 25 Finest Crime and Mystery Stories.*

Two acclaimed hardcover collections of her work have been published: *Too Many Tomcats* and (with her husband) *Murder — His and Hers.* The Collins's first novel together, the baby boomer thriller *Regener-*

ation, was a paperback best seller; their second collaborative novel, *Bombshell* — in which Marilyn Monroe saves the world from World War III — was published in hardcover to excellent reviews. Both are back in print under their "Barbara Allan" byline.

Barbara also has been the production manager and/or line producer on several independent film projects.

Max Allan Collins was named a Grand Master by the Mystery Writers of America in 2017. He has earned an unprecedented twenty-three Private Eye Writers of America "Shamus" nominations, many for his Nathan Heller historical thrillers, winning for *True Detective* (1983), *Stolen Away* (1991), and the short story "So Long, Chief."

His classic graphic novel *Road to Perdition* is the basis of the Academy Award–winning film. Max's other comics credits include "Dick Tracy"; "Batman"; his own "Ms. Tree"; and "Wild Dog," featured on the *Arrow* TV series.

Max's body of work includes film criticism, short fiction, songwriting, trading-card sets, and movie/TV tie-in novels, such as the *New York Times* best seller *Saving Private Ryan,* numerous *USA Today* best-selling CSI novels, and the Scribe Award–winning *American Gangster.* His nonfiction includes the current *Scarface and the Untouchable: Al Capone, Eliot Ness and the Battle for Chicago* (with A. Brad Schwartz).

An award-winning filmmaker, he wrote and directed the Lifetime movie *Mommy* (1996) and three other features; his produced screenplays include the 1995 HBO World Premiere *The Expert* and *The Last Lullaby* (2008). His 1998 documentary *Mike Hammer's Mickey Spillane* appears on the Criterion Collection release of the acclaimed film *noir, Kiss Me Deadly.* The Cinemax TV series *Quarry* is based on his innovative book series.

Max's recent novels include a dozen-plus works begun by his mentor, the late mystery-writing legend Mickey Spillane, among them *Murder, My Love* with Mike Hammer and the Caleb York western novels.

"BARBARA ALLAN" live(s) in Muscatine, Iowa, their Serenity-esque hometown. Son Nathan works as a translator of Japanese to English, with credits ranging from video games to novels.

The employees of Thorndike Press hope you have enjoyed this Large Print book. All our Thorndike, Wheeler, and Kennebec Large Print titles are designed for easy reading, and all our books are made to last. Other Thorndike Press Large Print books are available at your library, through selected bookstores, or directly from us.

For information about titles, please call:
(800) 223-1244

or visit our website at:
gale.com/thorndike

To share your comments, please write:

Publisher
Thorndike Press
10 Water St., Suite 310
Waterville, ME 04901